laid over

josie mae

For anyone who's ever had an airport crush.

chapter one

IN AN IDEAL WORLD, flights would never get canceled. There would never be a weather delay or a mechanical issue. Airlines would never be the reason someone missed something important, like a funeral or a birth.

But, unfortunately, we do not live in an ideal world. And even more unfortunately, I can't even blame the airline sometimes because it's simply not their fault. This exact moment is one of those cases—the only person I can take it up with is mother nature, and something tells me she's not interested in hearing what I have to say.

As I watch the snow fall outside, I know the flight cancellation is inevitable. I'm annoyed about it, for sure. But I also consider myself someone who has had pretty incredible flight karma. No previously canceled flights or missed connections, no accidentally sleeping through an alarm and frantically needing to rebook. And I'm classically someone who's pretty laid back, so getting worked up all because of something none of us could've avoided or planned for isn't really my deal.

However, I do wish the one time my flight was inevitably going to get canceled, it wasn't the one to my best friend's wedding.

My best friend, Hannah, moved to San Francisco a little over three years ago after college and met her perfect, sweet, charming, storybook boyfriend no less than a week together. They've been together ever since, happily working through milestones of first year together to moving in together to getting a dog together. The engagement came and then the visit where Hannah asked me to be her maid of honor and now—finally—the wedding.

Except I'm stuck here in Denver and the wedding festivities start tomorrow in San Francisco.

I cross my arms and look out the window, letting out an exhale through my nose. There are so many ways that this sucks—this is not the kind of storm I'm going to risk driving through, so I can't be the brave guest who literally did everything in my power to get there. The storm is probably going to make things *very* complicated in the airport for the next several days, meaning it won't be easy for me to get out of here. And possibly the worst of all is that I'm technically close to home, but I won't be able to get home because I can tell the snow is already piling up and my drive is too long to risk it.

"This already looks a lot worse than they said it would be on the news," a sweet-looking young couple says from next to me, pulling me out of my thoughts. They look at each other as the mom bounces her baby gently on her knee. "I'm going to call my mom and tell her she's going to need to dogsit again tonight."

"It'll be okay, let's just see if they cancel it first," her husband says, his tone comforting. She leans into his shoulder "Maybe it's a quick one. There must be some hope if they haven't canceled all of the other flights yet."

"Let's hope it's just delayed. I want to get home." She sighs as she looks out the giant windows at the planes.

I look around at everyone else. Everyone here has something they're trying to get to, whether it's just trying to get home or flying for a trip of some kind. We're fortunately outside of the window of traditional holiday travel now that it's mid-February, so things are a little less hectic. But it doesn't make it any less of an inconvenience to be stuck here.

I see a solo traveler, most likely college age, fully tuned into her phone with headphones over her ears. Nearby, a mom traveling with her toddler is trying to wrangle him in and keep his blanket off of the airport floor. An older couple across the way appears to be on FaceTime, smiling warmly into the camera and waving despite all of the chaos and uncertainty around them.

My eyes stop on a girl who looks to be about my age. She's on the floor in a corner, her laptop in her lap and a heavy looking book next to her. Her hair is claw clipped firmly to her head, pieces of hair falling into her face. I have to stop myself from staring at her and from thinking to myself—like some kind of idiot romantic interest in a teen movie—that she probably has no idea how effortlessly beautiful she looks in that moment.

It's a, frankly, ridiculous thought. I'm sure to a certain extent, she knows. She has to, with her deep brown hair and full lips that are currently pressed together because she's in thought about something on her computer screen. There's no way she doesn't look in the mirror and only ever think *okay, great—just as beautiful as I am every single other day*. Being able to look like that in an airport is a skill I can't comprehend.

I look away, focusing on the gate screen that tells us we're going to begin boarding in twenty minutes. Much like the young couple nearby, I'm kind of surprised nothing has been canceled or even delayed yet. It makes me think that maybe things aren't as bad on the radar as they seem out the window.

But even as I try to focus on the screen, I find myself stealing glances at the girl across the way. She's completely oblivions, headphones on while she works. She's perfect airport crush material—right there, but entirely inaccessible. Randomly the most beautiful person I've ever seen just going about her day.

I can't tell based on what she has with her if she's flying back home or away from home. Or maybe she's not from Colorado or San Francisco, and she's traveling between cities for some reason. I picture her as some sort of international traveler who's in the United States for work or for school. She has a cool British accent or something.

That's one of my favorite things about traveling—I've always loved people watching. I'm of the rare breed who genuinely likes being in an airport, which is also probably one of the reasons I'm not super anxious about what will happen next with our flight. As much as I'm upset about potentially being very late to my friend's wedding or missing it completely, there's nothing that can be done. There can't even be some kind of rescue mission because no one would be able to drive or fly to me. The best I can do is make peace with it, even though I know it'll be crushing once the crisis management part of me slips away and reality sinks in.

I look around and wonder if I've ever been someone's airport crush. I don't think there are any people in the running in this particular crowd—it feels like a lot of older couples and families. There are a few young guys, but I usually write them off. Even if I am their airport crush, it's not as much of an ego boost—or as fun to fantasize about—as a hot twenty-something woman who may or may not be queer.

I've been out for several years at this point, with one long term girlfriend and a few much less serious relationships over the course of that. I probably should've known sooner than freshman year of college considering I thought about most women in the same way I thought about this stranger in the airport. Women to me are beautiful, compelling, magnetic. I've always praised them extensively, painting very clear pictures of them when talking to people about them. All of the boys I had crushes on paled in comparison to the way I used to talk about the girls I was friends with before coming out. I still speak very highly of the women in my life, but there's a touch more self-awareness now that I've been out.

I've been single for a little over a year, which explains why I can't seem to take my eyes off the woman across the airport gate from me. I've had some sporadic luck here and there, but nothing long lasting. After trying out casual—flings and shitty dating app dates and flirting with people at bars—I got pretty badly burned by a month-long fling that ended with a *I don't think I'm looking for anything serious* a little bit ago and have since mostly been taking a break since then. That means it's been almost four months since a decent date and flirting and the feeling of kissing someone new.

I'd debated on really trying to go hard with finding a date to Hannah's wedding, but bringing a stranger to such a happy, love-filled day is so risky. I would spend the entire time so stressed about the other person and how well they mesh with the other guests at the wedding. I wouldn't want to bring a date to my best friend's wedding that my best friend can't stand—or one that I'm not even that serious about.

I'm extra relieved now that I didn't end up finding a date because I can't think of anything worse than getting trapped in an airport with someone who's just supposed to be a fun wedding date fling.

Getting stuck here with someone I do actually like, though, doesn't sound so bad. Uninterrupted time together, keeping each other company. My ex and I had ended because we just weren't that compatible in the long term and wanted different things. There's no shot of us ever getting back together, but I sometimes miss the familiarity.

I also, in the short term, miss going home with someone after a night out and the thrill of getting to know someone, figuring out how we work together. I definitely yearn for it, but it's been hard to find and I'm uninterested in diving deep into something with someone just because I'm craving some affection and connection. I want to really mean it.

But it does make it hard to be normal whenever I see someone attractive. It's like it lights up every part of my body, reminding me that even though I legitimately am okay with being single and I'm independent enough to handle it, I just want someone around from time to time. A vibrator and smutty novel can only get me so far. It can't replace the flirting and the touching and the chemistry. It can't replace pillow talk and falling asleep together, completely at ease, bodies tangled together.

I let out a small sigh. I really need to get laid. The situation is apparently more dire than I initially thought.

Maybe I can find someone at Hannah's wedding, but the odds of there being guests of our age I don't know personally in some capacity is fairly slim. And as much as I would love to be able to be family with Hannah, I don't know how she would feel if I went after one of her fiance's relatives.

I could try the San Francisco dating apps—maybe a few glasses deep on champagne I invite someone over to my hotel. I'll be there for a few days around the wedding, flying out there today so I can make it to the bachelorette party tomorrow and then the wedding and then sightseeing.

But I'm not sure casual is really what I'm looking for. All I've had is casual for so long; I'm not sure I want to keep getting myself into it when what I really want is something meaningful. I miss having a partner, not just someone to fool around with.

It's just been harder to find than I thought it would be. When I'm dating, it feels like a futile exercise in trying to connect with emotionally unavailable people. There are so many moving parts to making it work—general compatibility of personalities and interests, time and availability, mutual attraction. It's hard to believe sometimes that I was ever able to find a partner in general at one point in my life.

And then, on the reverse, I feel like I'm punishing myself for being single when I'm not dating. Taking time away from getting out there never feels that productive, probably because it's not a willing celibacy period. Choosing to get out of the game feels a lot better than being benched due to lack of possible partners.

It's all started to feel really...depressing, especially as of late. I try my best to not get in my head about it, but it's hard not to. I tend to pride myself on my ability to problem-solve and fend for myself. I've been successfully freelancing since I graduated from college, always hustling between graphic design contracts. I managed to relocate myself from my hometown to Colorado entirely on my own dime. I'm *accomplished*. Things are together for me.

But for some reason, I haven't been able to get things together in the dating realm. It's hard because partnership is one of the few things I can't fix for myself. No amount of journaling or problem solving will make a partner appear out of thin air.

Outside, the snow falls down even heavier than before. I pull out my phone and text Hannah: *Still not looking good. No cancellation—yet.*

Hannah quickly responded with a frowny face. I'm fortunate to have someone in my life who matches my mellow attitude so well. She's the exact opposite of a Bridezilla, desperate to make sure everyone around her is as happy as could be with the wedding. In this whole process, she's never lost sight of what really matters to her and only puts her foot down when she really feels like she needs to. The only thing she's had a serious opinion on so far has been the floral arrangements. Otherwise, she's happy when other people are happy.

It's the kind of peace that almost definitely comes from finding a man who makes an absurd amount of money working in tech. Planning a wedding suddenly becomes *much* easier with the support of a very hands-on wedding planner and a seemingly endless stream of cash. If Hannah wasn't one of the nicest people I've ever met, I would risk being bitterly jealous over how she's found love *and* financial stability. Instead, I can't help but think of how incredibly deserving she is for something like that to fall in her lap.

My phone vibrates and I look down, just as everyone else's phone around me also vibrates. It felt almost like watching a horror movie or disaster movie unfold in real time. I can immediately tell it's bad news.

"Flight 4441 to San Francisco has been canceled due to the weather. We apologize for the inconvenience. To rebook, please find the customer assistance desk at gate D34. To repeat: We cannot help you rebook here—please go D34," an attendant said over the gate speaker. She already sounds tired and over it. I'm sure she knows it's going to get ugly really quick.

Sure enough, the text message confirms the exact same thing. Our flight has been canceled and the airline is attempting to rebook us on the next flight out.

Groans and cries of frustration immediately fly out from the crowd.

"Fucking ridiculous," one guy next to me mumbles, wasting no time at all to leave the gate. He yanks his roller bag behind him as he departs.

I watch everyone else in the gate, trying to figure out what I'm supposed to do. My phone vibrates with another text and I see a message from my airline letting me know that they're unable to successfully rebook my flight. I'm going to have to go to customer assistance along with what appears to be everyone else in this part of the airport.

I sigh a little bit. Across the way, I see the girl slowly packing up her things. She doesn't seem particularly bothered by the announcement, but she might just have a really good poker face. Watching as she packs up, I can't help but admire her. I might as well steal the glances I can before she disappears into thin air like every other airport crush.

As I'm looking at her, her eyes suddenly pop up and lock with mine. I'm so flustered that I don't clock it immediately—I just continue to stare back at her, our gazes held in place. To my surprise, she flashes a small smile in my direction. She then drops her head back down toward the things she's packing up and picks herself up from the floor.

Embarrassed, I hurry off, choosing not to read too much into how the look she gave me felt distinctively flirty. It's definitely just me projecting and hoping she's into me.

I head over toward D34, where a line is rapidly growing. There are lots of people looking very stressed on the phone, negotiating with partners and parents and bosses on how they're going to get back. A couple of people try their best to keep their kids entertained, knowing it will probably be a long few hours of waiting to hear anything and many more hours before any of us are getting on a flight.

I step in line and pull out my phone to call Hannah.

Hannah answers in record time—the phone barely gets through a full ring before I hear her voice on the other end. "I got the text update," Hannah says before I can say anything at all.

"What text update?"

"I have flight notifications on for your flight," she says, like it's the most obvious thing in the world. I can hear the *duh* in her voice.

"Do you do that for all of my flights?" I ask.

"I love you, of course I do," Hannah says. "I watch the

flight tracker, too. If you crash in the woods somewhere, I will be the first one to report it and come looking for you."

"Right," I say. The thought of Hannah being in the woods in general, nonetheless the first person out on an expedition to a plane wreck, is laughable. But I don't doubt the genuine feeling behind the words. She's the sister I never had growing up in the same way I'm included as the fourth sister to her family. "I'm really sorry about the flight."

"It's okay, it's out of your control," she says. "This is what I get for scheduling a winter wedding. But I love February! It's my birth month and the month I met Alexander."

"And the month you ran into Paul Mescal that one time in London."

"Yes, exactly. You get me," she says. "And it was the only time slot for the rest of the year for the venue I wanted, so there's that too. But we'll figure it out, it'll be fine. There's time until the wedding. The most that'll probably happen is you'll miss the bachelorette."

"I can't miss the bachelorette," I said, my stomach sinking as reality begins to set in. Thinking about it theoretically didn't feel that terrible, but in practice, being late to Hannah's Wedding Week or completely missing it really bums me out. No matter how chill Hannah is capable of being, this is a once-in-a-lifetime moment. I can't miss it.

"It'll be okay, Harper. Seriously. As powerful as you are as a woman, you can't change the weather. This is exactly why we added some cushion time—there's always some kind of crisis that comes up," Hannah says. "See what you can do. And don't let them get away with not giving you a hotel voucher."

I chuckle. "Okay, okay," I say. Despite the light conversation, I can't shake the guilt I feel over potentially not being there as her maid of honor.

After hanging up, I put my phone away and look up ahead. The line in front of me is massive and moving slowly, all of us standing in the same spot for what feels like five minutes at a time. It's not looking good for any of us. I have a feeling it'll take at least an hour for me to be seen—realistically, probably longer than that.

"Missing a wedding?" a voice behind me asks.

I turn around, ready to make airport small talk—there's nothing else to be done when we're all going to be stuck standing so close together for the next few hours—when I'm suddenly stopped in my tracks.

The voice belongs to the girl from the gate earlier.

chapter two

I TRY to fight off the immediate nervous feeling that bubbles up in me. It's mortifying how quickly my body can fail me, turning me from someone fairly competent and capable into an absolute bumbling idiot whenever someone attractive is around. It's always been like that for me. It doesn't matter how many dates I go on or how confident I feel in myself; I always seem to completely lose all semblance of sanity in front of someone beautiful.

"Oh," I say, because there's nothing cooler than appearing surprised that your airport crush is talking to you. "Yeah. My best friend's getting married."

"That sucks, I'm sorry," she says.

A silence falls over us. I know I'm only aware of it because I'm acutely aware of how hot she is. She's even better looking up close. Her hair falls in loose strands around her face, framing her expressive, warm hazel eyes.

"What were you flying out for?" I ask, realizing a beat too late that it's polite to ask. I also, admittedly, don't want the conversation to end just yet. If I'm going to be stuck as hopelessly single, I need something to add some excitement to my life. The distraction also feels welcome considering the only thing I'm going to be doing in this line is wallowing in how guilty I feel about Hannah's wedding plans.

"Academic conference," she says.

"Oh, wow. That's cool," I say, genuinely meaning it.

"Yeah, not nearly as exciting as a wedding. I don't think I'm even that sad about missing it. This isn't a conference I'm that excited about—I just took it up because it's the most exciting location that I've been invited to," she explains. "Normally, the conferences are in, like...Cleveland. Which is totally fine and no offense to Ohio as a whole. But a break from the ultra cold weather and time in California sounds really nice."

"What were you supposed to present on?" I ask, as if I even completely understand what she means by an academic conference. I was in an art program—it came with its challenges, but it wasn't exactly *academically* challenging. It had been challenging in other ways instead, focusing on being able to create under pressure and take critique without taking it personally. I'm still working on the latter half of that.

"Symbolic interactionist theory and the family," she says. "Sociology stuff."

"That's cool," I say. "I don't think I know what any of those words mean."

She laughs and I can't help but smile a little bit to myself. It's the universal reaction to making someone attractive laugh. I'm immediately hooked and want to keep hearing it from her. "That's okay. Most people don't. Sometimes I'm not even sure I completely understand what I'm talking about or reading."

"It sounds important."

"Depends on who you ask. I like to think social science is one the greatest assets we can have in better understanding ourselves and others."

I'm immediately charmed. I can't help it. It's too early to feel this way but I already know could listen to her talk about anything for hours—read off a grocery list, narrate grass growing. I don't care.

"You must love it if you're willing to brave all of that schooling," I say and she cracks a smile. Her full lips pull back into a movie star smile. It's all so effortless on her. It's as though she literally wakes up being the most stunning woman in the world and then just goes about her business, acting completely cool about it.

She shrugs a little bit, her expression growing bashful. "I love it," she admits. "But it is boring to talk about—I'd rather hear about this wedding."

"I'm excited about it," I say. "I'm just hoping I can make it. I'm the maid of honor."

She flicks her eyes over me, an amused expression on her face. "Maid of honor?"

I think about my physical presentation—the short hair, the tattoos, the distinctively non-feminine clothing. Hannah and I have made at least a million jokes about it, trying to come up with something that feels a little more gender neutral. But I don't mind the title that much. It's exactly what we'd always talked about when we were little. And anyway, it is objectively funny to think of me as a maid of anything; I can't pass up the opportunity for the bit.

We share matching smirks of amusement. "Yeah," I say and she nods in appreciation.

"Wow," she says. "That is so exciting. I don't think I have any friends planning on getting married right now. But I also think that's part of being in academia. Being in a PhD program doesn't exactly allow time for things like serious dating, necessarily. I feel like I barely have time to remember to cook myself dinner."

I snort out a laugh and try not to think too hard about the fact that she's definitely single. That's only the first hurdle, anyway—it's not clear she's queer. The short nails and dressing like my friends implies a certain story, but that doesn't actually mean anything. I need single queer people to start writing on their foreheads *I'm single and queer* to make it at least a little bit easier on me. "I get it."

"Only a few more years and then I'll be a professor who ba," she says.

"You too can be completely demoralized by the working world," I say. I take what feels like a half-step forward in line as the line moves. It's truly a glacial pace—things continue to look very bleak in terms of reaching the customer assistance desk. I lower my expectations, hopeful now that I'll get up there within the next three hours. Even that feels like a stretch. "This is going to take forever."

"Part of me wants to just skip this whole thing completely and leave it up to the universe," she says. "I'm sure I can rebook on my own. If I don't go to my conference, so be it." She looks out the windows lining the wall across from us. "I am nervous about being able to get home, though. Not sure I like the idea of being snowed in at the airport."

"What, you don't want to have to sleep on the floor somewhere?"

"I was more imagining myself sitting upright in one of those chairs," she says, gesturing to the ones in a gate nearby. "Ideal sleep position. There's no way my back would hurt after that."

I laugh. "Oh, for sure."

"I'd make you watch my stuff for me while we sleep. We can pass off shifts," she says.

Her tone is light, but the thought of an implied future of any kind—even if that future is very literally just a few hours from now—makes my heart flutter. The second it registers that that's how I responded to her comment, I'm mortified. My face flushes and I have to look away, hoping she doesn't catch it.

I don't even know her *name* and she's managing to get me completely turned around. It's never been so obvious how badly I need to just get laid. Suddenly, getting back into the dating scene is sounding more appealing than it has in a long time.

Maybe this is what I need to finally cut my renewed desire for a relationship. Having a brief but debilitating crush on a random girl in an airport feels like a very quick way of curing myself of any desire to have a relationship. Isn't that what people always say—that it's the brief flings that have a way of stinging the most? If I only get this girl—beautiful, smart, fascinating—for a couple of hours, it might as well take me a few weeks to get over. Maybe rather than a girlfriend, I need my heart to get so crushed that I can't fathom dating ever again. Surely, that is the healthiest and most grown up way of approaching romance and there are no downsides.

"Brave of you to trust me to watch your stuff. We just met," I say, trying to match the lightness in her voice. I worry it comes across as forceful or mean, hyper aware of everything I'm saying and how it might be perceived. Embarrassingly, I want her to like me. But at least I'm self-aware enough to real-ize it.

"You seem trustworthy enough," she says and I'm certain I'm just making it up but part of me is convinced she's checking me out.

"I'm flattered," I say. "I'm not sure I'd trust you with my stuff—I'd probably sleep with one eye open the entire night," I say.

She cocks her head slightly to the side, her closed lips turning up in a smile. "Hmmm."

"What?" I ask. "Are you psychoanalyzing me right now? Don't read into what I just said."

"It's impossible not to when you're dropping such a juicy piece of information in my lap," she says. "But psychoanalysis is psychology. Sociology is focused on external forces. I'm more likely to theorize that your behavior is connected to your family or friends or hometown or whatever."

"That feels almost scarier to me somehow," I say. "Remind me not to mention anything to you about my parents."

That really gets her—she throws her head back in laughter. I smile in response, unable to help it. A burst of pride courses through me.

"I feel like that tells me everything I need to know," she says. She looks up at the line ahead and then around the airport. "I feel bad for all of the staff here. They're all about to have a very, very long shift."

"Yeah, I don't envy their job," I say. "I hope people are being nice to them."

She looks at me, her expression somewhat hard to read. But something in her eyes seems to be communicating curiosity at the very least. I'll take whatever I can get from her. "I'm Emmy, by the way," she says.

"Harper."

"Cute," she says. She smiles a little bit and I look away, knowing I'm going to blush again. I don't know what exactly is cute about it—my name? Me? It was just something she said because what else is there really to say in response to hearing someone's name?

"Do you think we'll be able to drive?" a woman behind us asks her husband.

"Oh, I don't think so," he says, shaking his head. "The radar isn't looking good. I don't think any of us are going anywhere anytime soon."

"Hm," the woman responds softly. She pauses and then directs her attention to us; I catch it out of the corner of my eye. "Excuse me—what are you young ladies doing?"

"Oh, don't bother them—they probably don't know anymore than we do," the husband says good-naturedly.

"I'm just running a little poll. I want to see what everyone else is doing so we can figure out what to do next."

Emmy and I turn to look at them. They look like they're a little older than my parents, with sweet, gentle expressions and soft voices.

"Not sure yet," Emmy says and looks at me. "Have you figured out a plan?"

I shake my head. I haven't even thought about what to do past the cancellation. All I know is that I'm currently stuck in the airport. Flights might be able to leave tomorrow, or it might take several days. I'm not really sure how to approach the situation.

"No," I admit. "I didn't calculate for any kind of delays in flying. I kind of assumed that things would go smoothly."

Emmy's lips perk up in an amused smile. "I think that's a reasonable assumption," she says. "Neither of us are sure what we're going to do. It doesn't look like there are any other flights leaving tonight, so we'll have to figure out what we want to do from here."

I try not to flush at her saying *we*. In any normal circumstance, I wouldn't think about it too much. But I like the implication that we're suffering through this together. I like the idea of her attaching herself to me, even if it's just to get through the next few hours.

"Are you from Denver?" I ask the couple. "If you leave now, you might be able to at least make it home before the snow gets too heavy."

Sleeping in the airport in general is pretty bleak, but the thought of this nice older couple getting stranded here with us feels wrong. I'm at the age where it's kind of a funny story to have to sleep in an airport somewhere waiting out a weather delay. I don't think I want to put them through that.

"No, this is our layover to get to California," she says. "We're from Maine."

"Far from home," I say.

"The weather isn't that different during certain times of year," the husband says.

"Fair enough," I say with a small smile. "What's bringing you out to California?"

"Our anniversary," the wife says with a smile. She turns to her husband. "Forty-five years. Can you believe that?"

"And we don't look a day over forty. Imagine that," the husband teases.

"Congratulations," Emmy says warmly. "What made you pick California?"

"Our honeymoon was in San Francisco. All Rosa had said about our honeymoon was she wanted to go as far from home as our money would allow us. It might not be Paris, but it was something really special," the husband says, presumably Rosa.

"I didn't leave him, so it must've been a pretty good vacation," Rosa teases.

The line moves up another couple of centimeters and we all adjust in line accordingly. As we're moving, Emmy's arm accidentally brushes against mine and it takes everything in me to be normal about it.

"How did you meet?" Emmy asks.

"Friends," Rosa says. "They said *you have to meet this guy Charlie. He's so funny.* And I was skeptical at first because what business do I have being with a guy where the first thing out of your mouth isn't *he's so handsome?*" she laughs and Charlie smiles good-naturedly; I can tell it's a joke they've been making for years. "But they were right—he was funny. And generous. And, it turned out, incredibly handsome, they'd just forgotten to fill me in on that part."

Looking at the way Rosa and Charlie look at each other and hearing how gentle they are with each other fills me with such an intense yearning it makes me almost feel sick. I've always considered myself someone who can keep my head on pretty straight with romance and I never prioritize it over anything else. But lately, I have *really* been craving connection. It's gotten so bad that I had to ban Tyler Childers in my house, unable to listen to someone singing about how deeply in love he is with the woman in his life.

"That's so sweet," Emmy says and I wait for her to mention something about a partner at home that she's also deeply in love with. I keep bracing myself for the inevitable crushing disappointment that will follow. She's just an airport crush and it's all temporary, but she's still a crush. She's something to put *some* amount of hope in.

That's how I know I'm really and truly single. I don't even have a crush, so I have to project a crush on someone I don't know. Embarrassing.

"And you two are also together?" Rosa asks.

It takes me a second to process what she's asking. "Oh!" I cry, laughing. "We're not—"

"We just met, actually," Emmy says, her response much more level than mine. She laughs kindly. "Does it seem like we're together?" She turns to me, offering me a smile that nearly brings me to my knees. It makes me want to go *we are together! Whatever she needs from me, I'll give her!*

Rosa blushes. "This is mortifying—I'm so sorry. I thought you two were traveling together and...oh, dear," she says and laughs, hiding her face in her hands.

"Our daughter is a lesbian—I think we're projecting a little bit," Charlie admits with a chuckle. He looks between us, his eyes landing on me. "She's about your age. And she actually kind of looks like you."

"I hope that's a compliment," I say.

"Not a completely off-base projection, either," Emmy says and it feels like a jolt of electricity is coursing through me. The comment is so bold that I'm certain that I'm mishearing her or misunderstanding her. Maybe the part of it that wasn't off-base was clocking that she's queer and that's all that she's implying.

But with her brushing the tiniest bit against me, I'm realizing that maybe she does actually mean it. Maybe she's realizing the same thing that I am—that we only have so much time together here and we probably have to go bold if we want anything to happen.

"Not off-base for me, either," I say quietly. I like the plausible deniability of it; I'm a lesbian, so it's true that their guess isn't entirely inaccurate. And I'm also very much into Emmy, so if she's implying that she's into me, we can be on the same page.

She turns to me and we share the kind of smile I would write about in my diary if I'd kept one beyond elementary school. Our eyes linger on each other for a second and, against my better judgment, I'm picturing a future together. I can see a whole night playing out together—we stay up all night, talking and getting to know each other. We board our shared flight, exchanging numbers in the baggage claim with promises that we'll see each other when we're both back in Colorado. There would be dates and an end to the dating deadzone I've been in.

I know it's stupid. Even as I'm thinking it, I know how impractical it is and how there's no shot it will actually happen that way. Things like that don't happen to me. They happen in the movies, but I'm just some normal twenty-five-year-old who happened to have her flight canceled. It doesn't mean anything spectacular or life changing is going to come of it.

But still, I can't help but hold onto the hope. It feels kind of good to let myself get caught up in something again. Even if it'll be short lived, it's a nice reminder that I'm capable of still getting swept away in my feelings. I can still have a crush, still be intrigued by someone. There are so many people out there who I have yet to meet, so many new crushes I can have. If I have myself half-convinced that this stranger and I are going to fall in love in an airport, I can definitely crush hard on someone else.

Part of me feels a weird connection to Emmy specifically, though. Even though I know in the back of my head that this isn't a logical crush, I'm really intrigued by her. She's beautiful and kind. I'm getting just enough pieces of her to want to know more. Even if I could have a crush with any random stranger in the world, I kind of want it to be her.

I push the thought of my head. Now *that* is a truly insane thing of me to think.

"Do you think the snow will lighten up enough for any flights to go out tonight?" I ask.

"I'm skeptical," Charlie responds.

"Me too," Emmy says. "I haven't been in Colorado for very long, but all it takes is a couple of winters to know when it's *really* snowing."

"How long ago did you move here?" I ask.

"About two years ago," she admits. "If you're a native to the area, ignore any commentary I have on the weather here. I'm from Arizona, so I don't know snow like this really."

I laugh. "Don't worry, I'm not from here either. I can't tease you for being a transplant."

"Hm," Emmy responds thoughtfully, and the only thing I can think is it feels a little bit like we're microdosing a date. It's like I'll get just a little bit of her here and there—just enough to want to ask more questions. If we were meeting at a party instead of an airport, I would have found a way to ask for her number—or at least, ask a friend of a friend if she's single. I would've done everything I could to gauge if I should ask her on a date, wanting to know more about her.

Part of it is an exercise in curiosity—she's beautiful, so it makes sense I want to get to know her and see if we're compatible beyond the surface level conversation skills. But I also know my tendency is to want to know as much as I can as quickly as possible so I can make a snap judgment. One of the things I struggle the most with is being so quick to not see things through. Sometimes it feels like I'm really picky—too picky, maybe. But other times it feels like logical preservation. Some people aren't going to be a good match and it's obvious by the end of a first date. It can even be obvious within the first ten minutes of conversation.

So far, I've only come to like her more—something that can always change, but the lesbian instinct to U-haul is unfortunately strong, especially in conditions like this. Getting snowed in somewhere together is inherently romantic; it feels like the kind of stuff that should be in a romantic comedy.

"Oh, look—they're canceling more flights. I don't think anyone is leaving tonight," Emmy says, pointing to a screen nearby that displays the departing flights. It's lighting up with all sorts of newly updated cancellations—it looks like they're anticipating no more flights will be leaving for the rest of the day. As Emmy points, she leans near me, close enough that I can feel the body heat radiating from her. Her red pullover sweatshirt brushes against my arm.

"Guess we might as well get comfortable," Rosa says. Her husband puts an arm around her and pulls her in for a hug. I can tell from her expression how hard she's trying to put on a brave face about it.

It occurs to me, then, that I'm sad too. I've been clinging onto hope that maybe it wouldn't be that bad—the weather has a way of quickly turning, snowstorms stopping suddenly or snow not falling as heavily as originally predicted. And being in an area that's used to snow means the airport staff is prepared to fight against bad weather. But no matter how prepared an airport is, sometimes the weather does just suck. And it makes it even worse when no one could've predicted how bad it was going to be.

"Did you realize it was going to get this bad?" I ask.

Emmy shakes her head. "I had no idea. I wouldn't have bothered coming here if I'd known. I wouldn't have minded being home with my cat instead of here."

"Cat mom," I say, a light tease to my voice.

"He's my pride and joy," she says and pulls out her phone and shows me her lockscreen wallpaper. A sweet black cat with giant eyes looks back at me.

"He's so cute," I say. "How old is he? He looks tiny."

"Only about a year, but he's also small for his age," she says. She puts her phone away. "His name is technically Buster but I usually just call him baby. I don't think he knows his actual name."

We briefly lock eyes for a moment, the sound of her saying *baby* bouncing around in my head. Even though it wasn't directed at me, it might as well have been with the way I'm responding to it.

"I don't have any pets but I want to get one eventually," I say. "It sounds pretty intense—I think I need a little more stability before that. Maybe a co-parent"

"He's a lot of work, honestly. Adopting him completely turned my life inside out. He might as well be a baby," she says, nodding knowingly.

We inch up again in the line and I resist the urge to check the time—I know it'll only depress me. When I look back down the line and up toward the front, I can see that we've barely moved.

Although, admittedly, being stuck here with Emmy makes me kind of wish the line didn't have to eventually end. I'm already not looking forward to having to go our separate ways. I like living in this little fantasy bubble of being able to crush on her without really, actually getting my heart broken. She'll always just be the beautiful stranger I met in the airport that one time during a snowstorm. Someone to romanticize, to think back on the what ifs. It sounds a little more appealing than having to put myself out there and risk yet another failed attempt at a genuine relationship. But then again, maybe I'm just avoidant.

"Hi everyone—we are unable to rebook any flights leaving tonight. We—" an airport employee says as she walks down the line of people waiting to be seen by customer assistance. The entire crowd simultaneously lets out a groan, cutting her off in the middle of the start of her next sentence. She raises her voice slightly over the crowd. "I'm sorry for the inconvenience. I know this isn't ideal. We ask that you hang tight. The storm is expected to pass overnight and flights should be back tomorrow. You will be automatically rebooked onto a flight sometime soon—we're just waiting for the system to catch up."

"Oh, wow," Rosa says with a slight sigh. She turns to Charlie and he puts his arm around her, rubbing his hand into her shoulder.

"Sorry about your anniversary trip," Emmy says softly. I can tell she means it.

Rosa looks at her husband, her hand on his chest. "It doesn't really matter where we're celebrating it. All that matters is we get to celebrate together."

"Sappy," Charlie teases.

Emmy and I exchange a small smile, silently asking each other *isn't this so cute?* And it is. It reminds me of how badly I want that kind of relationship. I sometimes worry that I'm a little too free spirited or hard to please to truly settle down, but I know that the way I crave stability and monogamy is genuine. Just because I've had a hard time finding a partner doesn't mean I don't want one; it just means I'm not willing to make space for one who isn't everything and more to me.

Rosa laughs, feigning an eyeroll. "Should we go get a hotel room in the area before everyone books the place out?"

"Definitely. I'm too old to sleep in these seats," Charlie

says. He takes Rosa's overhead roller bag into his hands and looks at me and Emmy. "It was lovely to meet you ladies. Good luck with your travels."

Rosa stops in her tracks, turning to us before heading off. "Are you planning on getting a room?"

"Oh, I'm living off of a grad student salary," Emmy says. "I can't afford that."

"You two should consider splitting one—spare yourselves the experience of sleeping here if you can," she says. "Money will come back but back pain is forever."

"And we should know," Charlie agrees.

I blush at the thought. There's no way in hell I'm getting a hotel room with Emmy for a whole long list of reasons—the number one being that I don't trust myself to be cool about splitting a hotel room with her. There's no way I'll be able to sleep knowing that we're alone together somewhere so private. I'll be so worried about snoring or saying something embarrassing or doing something embarrassing.

"Maybe we will," Emmy says with a polite smile, telling me that she's also not planning on taking Rosa's guidance.

Rosa smiles a little bit, looking between the two of us. For a second, I feel like she can read my mind and knows exactly how I've been thinking about Emmy. I worry that it's written all over my face—the way I can't seem to take my eyes off of her, the way everything she says is of interest to me. It's so plainly a crush that I'm sure Rosa can sense it. And if Rosa can sense it, I wonder if Emmy can too. And the possibility of her piecing it together makes me want to curl up in the snow outside and hide forever.

Rosa gives us a sweetly maternal look. "Take care, ladies."

"You too," I say and Emmy waves goodbye.

With the buffer gone, I feel suddenly very aware of how it's just me and Emmy again. It's like every single thought I could ever produce escapes me. My brain cannot develop even one full sentence. I can't think of a pivot to get me out of thinking about sharing a hotel room with Emmy. I worry if I think about it for too long, my thoughts will verge on wildly inappropriate and I can't handle that. The last thing I need is to think about is how soft Emmy's skin probably is and how full her lips are and what it would sound like to hear her say my name...

"Should we get a drink?" Emmy offers. "I don't know if standing in line is really going to benefit us at all. We might as well stick it out elsewhere."

There's no way alcohol will make this any easier for me. It might soothe my nerves, but it will also *definitely* amplify my attraction. I already know my thoughts about how hot I think she is are going to be all-consuming. No shot I'll be able to be on my best behavior.

But I can't give up this chance.

"Uh, yeah. Definitely. Let's do it," I say, surprised that she asked but glad that she did. I'm also surprised by how easily the words pour out. Even if I'm nervous about how I'll behave, I'm not an idiot. If a beautiful girl wants to go get a drink, I will get a drink with her.

"Okay, great," Emmy says and smiles at me in a way that tells me I'm about to get myself into so much trouble.

chapter three

THE AIRPORT IS in a state of chaos I've never seen before. Even holiday flights I've taken in the past are nothing compared to what's unfolding right now. There are people on frantic phone calls, people crying, kids running laps around gates as their parents try their best to coordinate over a shared phone screen. It's only gotten worse as time passes and more flights are canceled.

We step to the side, letting the crowds around us rush by in a hurry. We haven't figured out what options we have for a drink or where we want to go, but I'm so overwhelmed by the number of people that it's hard to think.

"Rosa and Charlie have the right idea booking a hotel for the night now," I admit. "This place is already a zoo."

"I know. Have you ever gotten snowed in here? I know they have, like, cots and things but..." Emmy says, looking around. She looks at the airport map and nods to herself like she's made a decision. She turns to look at me and I nod, following alongside her and letting her take the lead.

"No, this is all a new experience for me," I admit. "Starting to realize what everyone means when they talk about how much they hate traveling."

"Real," Emmy says. "Part of the experience, though, I think. All of the mishaps are what makes it interesting. It'd be too boring if travel always went exactly how it was supposed to."

"Very positive spin on things," I say.

We approach a standard airport restaurant and bar. It's busy but not as busy as I'd expect it to be, probably because it's such a strange inbetween time for a meal. With all of the flight delays we've already dealt with, our flight that was supposed to be a comfortable mid-morning flight has kept us at the airport until mid-afternoon. It's just past lunch but it's still too early for dinner. And even for an airport, it's an odd time to get a drink.

I look around, wondering how widespread flight cancellations are beyond our airline. It seems like some of the airlines are still holding out hope for their evening flights.

She laughs and shrugs easily. "I guess I tend to fall on the pretty positive side of things," she says. She glances over at me. "I mean, if our flight didn't end up getting delayed, we probably never would've met. Now, we have a great story to tell everyone when we're finally able to leave the airport. This is way more exciting than making it to our destination and being like *yeah, just another flight.*"

"Yeah, for sure," I say, trying to be as casual as possible but failing dramatically.

I take a deep breath, forcing myself to be so incredibly chill about what she just said. There's nothing to read into; she's just simply making an observation. It entirely makes sense that she'll mention me when people ask her about her experience getting snowed in at the airport.

But there's something so strange about permanently being part of her life. She's essentially a stranger to me, but this is also the kind of thing we'll probably always remember. Nothing even that romantic or dramatic has to happen for that to be the case. I'm sure I'll think about her for the rest of my life whenever I'm in an airport, even just in passing. It'll probably be the same for her. It's just how it goes; certain people, even strangers, can be so memorable from quick interactions.

"For two," I say when the waitress approaches. She nods and walks us over to an empty table.

"I'll give you a minute to look over the menus," she says. I can see in her expression that she's trying her best to be cheery for us, but I'm assuming she's also very aware of the weather. I can't imagine the prospect of getting stuck here because of a work shift is appealing.

"Thank you," Emmy and I say simultaneously. The waitress walks away and I study the menu, debating on if I'll just get a drink or if I'll get something to snack on too.

"Some people would say a boring flight is a good thing," I say with a slight smile, going back to our earlier conversation. "Who knows—maybe we were going to meet anyway. Maybe we were supposed to be seated next to each other."

"I personally never make small talk with the people I sit near on a plane," Emmy admits.

"That actually surprises me a little bit considering you were so open to chatting with me in line," I say. It comes out flirtier than I intend for it to. But then again, maybe the time I'm spending with Emmy is making me feel bolder around her. The more natural form of my personality—the one that isn't afraid to be loud and bold—is slipping out as I forget just how hot Emmy is.

She shrugs coyly. "We were going to potentially be stuck in that line for hours. What else was I supposed to do?" she says. "And pass up the opportunity to another young, presumably queer person? No way."

My jaw drops as I laugh, surprised by her comment. "How did you clock me?"

"Are you serious? The haircut, the short nails, the clothes," she says, gesturing to me. Her eyes sparkle playfully. "I can read it off of you a mile away. And I knew I'd probably have to say something first because I know I look like I'm straight."

I bark out a laugh. "You don't look straight—"

"I dress exactly like any girl with a TikTok account and a love for Taylor Swift. I might as well have some guy on call who I've been in an on-and-off situationship for months. It's okay—you don't have to pretend it isn't true. It's a very specific brand of femme and it is straight-coded."

"I had a feeling you might be."

"Straight?"

"No!" I laugh. "Queer. But I was also thinking it might just be wishful thinking." The comment comes out before I fully think it through. And by the time I realize what I'm saying, it's way too late to take it back. Internally, I scramble for some kind of explanation but I know there isn't one. That's the kind of thing people only say when they're flirting.

Emmy opens her mouth, about to respond, when the waitress comes back over. "Can I get you anything to start?"

"Oh, sure. Um. I'll have a vodka soda," Emmy says.

"Tequila sour," I say.

"Coming right up," the waitress says and turns on her heel.

As the waitress walks away, I try to think of some kind of topic I can switch to so I don't have to navigate what's to come. I'm not the kind of person who usually just throws out lines and hopes the other person will pick up interest. I'd rather die keeping my crush a secret than be bold enough to make some kind of first move.

Or at least, that's how I normally am. But apparently, my mouth had different plans today.

"So, where are you from before moving to Colorado—"

"You're not changing the topic on me," Emmy says,

leaning forward over the table. She locks eyes with me and I blush so deeply my cheeks are burning. "What do you mean by wishful thinking?"

"Oh, I just—"

"Answer the question, Harper. Inquiring minds want to know," she says, her tone playful. But there's undeniable subtext. I can hear it in the low hum of her voice, see it in her expression.

I've always been a pretty capable flirt. I usually love putting myself out there and getting to know new people. A lot of the time, it's not even that intentional. I just like *talking*. I've always found it fun to ask people questions and genuinely get to know them, which can sometimes come across as more than platonic.

But Emmy is really rattling me. The combination of someone being bold and beautiful is something I'm not used to. Usually, people aren't able to beat me at my own game of flirting for fun.

I tap my fingers against my leg, hoping she can't tell that she's making me nervous. But based on the way she's keeping her eyes fixed on me, I think she has to know that I am.

"It's...stupid," I say.

"It's not."

I shrug a little, looking down at the table. "You're, like, the token airport crush or whatever. You were the hot person at my gate for me to fixate on. It makes the game less fun to imagine that you're straight and would never be interested in me. Hence, projecting and...wishful thinking."

"I'm your airport crush?" Emmy teases.

"Oh, please," I say, laughing. I hide my face in my hands. "It's...ignore me. Whatever. I'm so embarrassed."

"No, don't be," she says, reaching out and gently pulling my hands away from my face. "What exactly is an airport crush?"

"Wait, you don't know?"

She shakes her head. "I've never heard of that before."

"It's...I don't actually know how to explain it. It's just, like, a random hot person you find in the airport. Someone at your gate who you're convinced is the most attractive person you've ever seen—"

"I'm the most attractive person you've ever seen?"

"You're distracting me," I say, laughing. "It's just a fantasy. Hot people seem even hotter than normal in an airport for some reason. I don't know what the science is behind it. All I know is that it's part of the travel experience."

"Hm," Emmy says, nodding to herself. "Maybe I should find a way to write a paper on this for one of my classes."

"Only if you credit me."

"Oh, of course. Leading expert on airport crushes."

"Someone has to be."

Emmy leans forward. "It turns out the leading expert in airport crushes is my airport crush," she says. "What are the odds?"

"Yeah, yeah—"

"I mean it, why else would I spark up a random conversation with you in line? To make nice with a random stranger for no personal gain?" she jokes.

I shake my head, smiling. I can't help but feel completely blown away by her. I feel like I'm running a marathon trying to keep up, the cobwebs being dusted off of the part of my brain that has forgotten what it feels like to have a crush.

"You're just saying that because we're discussing airport crushes. You didn't even know what it was until a few seconds ago," I say.

"I felt that you were my airport crush, I just didn't have a name for it yet," she says.

The waitress approaches with our drinks, placing them down on our table. "Any food?"

"I need a little bit more time to look over the menu," Emmy says.

"Perfect. I'll swing back around in a little bit," the waitress says before heading off again.

I look up at Emmy, who's casually scanning over the menu as if she didn't just drop a game changing piece of information into my lap. I'm starting to think that she really *is* beating me at my own game. She's just as skilled at flirting as I am and doesn't mind doing it for sport.

But part of me is hoping that it's not just because it's fun to flirt and be hot. I really, earnestly want her to like *me* specifically.

"Are you getting anything to eat?" Emmy asks, still so casual. I don't know how she can feel even the tiniest bit normal under these conditions; I feel like I'm about to have a heart attack.

"I'm considering," I say. "I guess I'll have to plan my meals accordingly tonight, since the restaurants will eventually close."

"Have your eye on any part of the airport floor yet for sleeping?" she asks. "Terminal D seems to have some pretty cushy space."

I snort out a laugh. "Do you really think you're going to be able to sleep? It doesn't seem like it'll be comfortable. I'm unfortunately one of those people who can't sleep anywhere. I can barely sleep on flights."

"If I'm tired enough, definitely," she says. "And if you hold me all night long, of course."

I nearly choke on my drink. "Oh, of course," I say. When she turns her head away, I take bigger gulps of my drink, desperately needing to lose my inhibitions if I'm going to get through this.

And sure enough, flirting starts to feel a tiny bit easier. I'm even more aware of how badly I want to get laid and how hot the woman in front of me is, but I also feel less worried about myself in all of it.

I feel just a little bit less in my head, a little bit more capable of just leaning into the moment. Maybe I'll end up embarrassing myself and maybe it'll get weird and we'll never speak again. But that's probably going to happen no matter what, anyway. She's the perfect person to be completely at ease with. We'll probably never run into each other and it'll never go beyond this, so there's no point in holding back. It's kind of an ideal one night stand situation. Suddenly, I see the appeal of the people who have short-term vacation flings.

"You never answered my question about where you're from," I say.

"I can't believe you actually want to get to know me. Can't you just tell me over drinks how pretty I am and how sad it is that we're crossing paths in such a transitory way?"

"We'll get there eventually. Let me wine and dine you first."

Emmy snorts out a laugh. "Small suburb in Illinois. I grew up, like, a couple of hours outside of Chicago."

The waitress came back over. "Can I get you guys anything?"

"Order of fries?" I offer, looking at Emmy. She nods enthusiastically. "We'll split an order of fries for now. Thank you." The waitress nods and heads off and I turn to look at Emmy again. "How was it? Your hometown, I mean."

"Fine enough. Not much to report on. It's the kind of place where when I told my parents I was leaving for college, they didn't even try to argue with me about it. They love it there but I also think they acknowledge it's pretty...one note. They'd just been craving something different from a city. They both wanted a backyard."

"Why do they live there?"

"Very classic stuff—they both grew up there, met as children, fell in love as teenagers. They tried out city living for a little bit before deciding they weren't interested in raising a family somewhere so cramped. They ended up buying a house not far from where both sets of their parents lived and then a few years after that, gave birth to me and my brother. I went to Michigan for undergrad and then came to Colorado for grad school. My parents don't really get me wanting to leave and build a life somewhere else, probably because they tried it and didn't like it that much, but they're supportive."

"That's sweet," I say.

"Yeah, I'm fortunate they haven't guilted me out of doing what I want to do. It would be easy for them to make me feel bad about wanting to leave. And I do feel bad about it some-times, it's just..."

"Not enough to live there," I say.

"Exactly."

I take a sip of my drink. "I get it. My parents were happy to push me out of the nest or whatever, but I feel bad about leaving them behind. It's just me, so they immediately became empty nesters when I started college. I think my mom was hoping I might fail—or at least flounder a little bit—when I started freelancing after college so I'd have to move back home, but things have lined up really well. I'm not making, like, a *lot* of money by any means, but I can afford to have my own room. Even if it's in a house of four people. And kind of in the middle of nowhere."

"That's really good," Emmy says. "I'm sure they're proud."

The waitress walks back over and drops off the fries. Emmy and I don't hesitate to dive in.

"I think they are," I say. "It's hard moving away but I knew it was either that or spending my entire life wondering what it would've been like. I told myself that I'd give myself the year and if I hated it, I'd go back."

"Oh, I knew without question that I was never going back. I had no other option," Emmy admits. "I couldn't do it. I know it's not a failure to not be able to settle away from your hometown, but I view it as a personal failure for myself. It'd be letting myself down." She looks at me. "Where's home for you?"

"Outside of Austin."

"Oh, wow. Texas girl. Yeehaw."

I snort out a laugh. "Kind of—my parents are both transplants so I kind of feel like a transplant, too. I was raised with the influence of their parents and their hometowns more than anything else."

Emmy dives in for another fry, dipping it into the ketchup and then the mustard she had poured out onto the parchment paper. I smile a little bit watching her do it, curious where the habit began. I've never seen someone eat their fries that way, but I think it's cute. "Have you ever been to a rodeo?"

I laugh. "I have, actually. Are there rodeos in Illinois?"

"If there are, I never went to any. Or heard about them. But I was too busy being a Tumblr angsty teen type to pay attention to any part of rural living. Everything in my life always centered around wanting to get out and do something else. I always knew I'd end up in a city eventually."

"Is Denver the city for you permanently or are you going to try and go bigger?" I ask. Denver is still a hike from me—I'm based in a much smaller town outside of the city—but I'm relieved she's at least within the same state as me.

"I don't know yet," she admits. "I like it out here, but I liked the program mostly. I don't know if I can handle something like New York or Los Angeles. I'm using this conference as an excuse to explore a little of San Francisco and see if that's more my speed."

I nod, surprised by how sad I am to hear that Colorado might not be forever for her. It's stupid to mourn a theoretical move before she's even gone, especially because she's a stranger. But gut feeling can also say a lot and my gut feeling is telling me that Emmy is someone I don't want to lose sight of.

"Can I be honest with you?" she says. "I'm kind of envious of my parents. I feel like I've always, like, *wanted* something. My entire life has been built around the desire for more. I'm always looking for the next thing. But my parents are just so...happy. They have this beautiful life surrounded by family in a place they love. They work just, like, normal people jobs and make normal people money and do normal people things."

"Do you think you're not a normal person?"

Emmy thinks on it for a second. "I feel like I'm too hard to please, almost. I'm chasing some kind of goal that I don't think is actually obtainable. And I think, somewhere deep in me, I actually do have the desire for a stable home and partner and backyard."

Even though it's not the same context, I feel a warm buzz in my chest at her mentioning that she feels like she's hard to please. There's something so comforting about hearing her express the same thing that I feel.

I nod. "I think it's normal to feel that way on both fronts. I think that's kind of what it's all about. We have all of these things we could do and could want, but we have to figure out what we want to pursue. Maybe you'll hate living in a city and end up back in your hometown in two years. Or maybe you'll realize New York was the perfect fit for you all along. Or maybe you're meant to be in Europe somewhere."

Emmy smiles a little bit. "You're the first person who I think actually kind of gets it. I think so many of my friends and family members are so nervous for me. They don't get that I *like* the uncertainty. For now, at least. I think deep in my core, I want something stable one day. But they don't get that

I can kind of want both things and change my mind as time goes on."

"Yeah—" As I reach for the plate of fries again, my hand bumps Emmy's glass and it knocks over onto the table. It all happens simultaneously too quickly and too slowly. I see everything, but I can't seem to stop it. Before I know it, her sweatshirt is drenched with her vodka soda. I gasp, reaching for napkins. "I'm so sorry. Holy shit."

"It's okay," Emmy says, laughing. She dabs at the sweatshirt. "At least it was something clear."

"No, I'm really so sorry. I'm so embarrassed," I say and suddenly, the image of me and Emmy spending the rest of the day—and then maybe time after our flights—together vanishes. Theoretically, something spilled on someone else seems like a cute meet cute but in reality, it's mortifying.

"It's okay. Really, Harper. Don't stress it. I have my overhead, so I can just change into something else."

"Do you want me to order you another drink?"

"No, I'll take this as a sign from the universe I'm risking a violent hangover if I keep drinking and then attempt to sleep in the airport," she says.

"Some would say alcohol would probably make the evening go by a lot faster."

"Maybe I don't want it to go by faster," she says with a slight teasing smile.

I fight the blush warming my cheeks. "Do you want to go change? I can hold down the table," I say.

"No, it's okay. I can wait," she says. She pulls her sweatshirt over her head and I realize it's soaked through to the shirt underneath. It clings to her chest and stomach—not as badly as it did with her sweatshirt, but definitely still a fair amount.

My guilt mixes with unfiltered, gut-reaction arousal to such a degree that I actually have to look away. The shirt she's wearing isn't anything particularly wild or sexy; it's just a plain t-shirt. But the way it sits against her frame makes my heart race. Her nipples are visible through her shirt, telling me she isn't wearing a bra.

There's a hot rush between my legs I haven't felt in what feels like ages. The combination of her being so sexy and beautiful and easy to talk to is hitting me from every angle. Without question, I know I'm deeply, irreversibly attracted to her.

I flag down the waitress, still feeling terrible about soaking Emmy's sweatshirt but also kind of grateful I got to see what's underneath.

"Can we have the check please?" I ask.

"Of course," the waitress says and disappears. I finish off my drink and Emmy pulls her damp shirt away from her skin.

"I'm really so sorry," I say.

"Stop! You're fine," Emmy says, laughing. "It's funny. And it's not like we have anything better to do than deal with my wet clothes. It's an activity."

I smile, charmed by how damn *cute* she is. The more I get to know her, the more certain I am that she might actually be sunshine personified.

The waitress drops the check off and I quickly pay while Emmy protests in the background.

"Let me Venmo you," she says.

"I said I was going to wine and dine you. Part of that is me paying," I say.

"I'm buying you something else later, then. I hope you like ice cream."

"Why does that feel almost threatening?"

After paying, we gather up our things and leave the restaurant. I look around for signs toward a nearby restroom.

"This way," I say and we start walking through the crowds of people again. Things seem to have slowed down pretty significantly—no one is really rushing anymore since there's nothing to really rush *to*. It's either people making the decision to drive somewhere or go to a hotel or stay put for the night. Based on the number of announcements being shared over the airport intercom, the rest of the flights going into the evening have been canceled.

"There's a family one in case you need more space to lay out your suitcase," I offer.

"Perfect," Emmy says when we stop in front of the bathroom door. She steps toward it, knocking and then pulling the door open when no one answers from inside. As she steps in, pushing her bag inside, she turns to look at me, flashing me a look through her eyelashes. "Aren't you coming?"

chapter four

MY MOUTH INSTANTLY GOES DRY. Every part of my body heats up, turning to fire. She keeps her eyes fixed on me as she waits for a response but I can't articulate anything. Instead, I silently walk toward her. Our bodies brush as I step into the bathroom, sealing my fate.

The moment makes me feel almost out of body. It's entirely surreal—me somehow in this bathroom, the two of us alone. The heavy implication of the two of us being here together. She could've easily had me stand outside. In fact, that probably would've been the most reasonable course of action.

But instead, she invited me in. And now we're here.

Emmy doesn't seem phased in the same way I am. She moves to her bag, dropping it gently to the ground and undoing the zipper. The sound of a zipper had never been particularly erotic to me until now. I'm realizing just how intimate it feels, the way it makes me think of undoing the pants of another person.

I can't tell where I'm supposed to fix my eyes; if I should be looking at her or looking somewhere else. There isn't much to see in the bathroom we're in. It's exactly what a family airport bathroom would look like—more spacious than a standard stall with a diaper changing station. No frills. All white tile and bad lighting.

But with the way my body is acting, it might as well be the honeymoon suite. Mentally, I'm preparing for something to happen—anything at all. I can feel wetness between my legs at the thought of Emmy's lips finding mine, my hands down her cute, extremely flattering sweatpants. I think about us fucking, going round after round until someone inevitably comes to knock on the door to actually use the family bathroom.

My gaze falls on Emmy's back as she squats on the floor, going through her bag for a shirt. She's carefully sorting through everything. From where I'm standing, it looks like she keeps a neatly packed bag. Everything is sorted carefully and everything has its place. Her motions are delicate and not rushed.

It occurs to me that she really must not be phased in the same way I am. I don't know how she's not affected by the intimacy of this moment. I'm so aware of everything—where I stand, how much I'm breathing and how loud it is, what to do with my hands. I don't want her to think I'm bored standing here with her, but I also don't want her to think I'm nervous. That doesn't exactly up my cool factor.

Maybe she's not nervous because she does stuff like this all the time. She's able to do casual in a way that I've never seemed able to master. Hannah says it's because I have an earth sign venus in my astrological chart; I can do casual to a certain extent, but once there are any thoughts about a future, it's off to the races. I've never been able to have a normal crush and slow burns make me anxious. When it comes to meeting a partner, I feel like I've always just *known*. And there's something about Emmy that makes me think there has to be more to this than just some girl in the airport.

But then again, it could be wishful thinking. Wishful

thinking about her being queer was one thing, but this is about feelings. It's about mutual interest and attraction. Anyone can fuck once, but it's an entirely different combination of things that leads to people actually liking each other.

It feels like we've both been silent for at least fifteen minutes even though I know it's only been a minute or two since the door clicked shut. My heart is beating so quickly and my palms are so sweaty someone would probably assume I was in danger if they were looking at my vitals.

Emmy stands up, a shirt pulled from her suitcase and draped out on top of her other things. The tag of her wet sweatshirt is laced over the purse hook on the door. My mind is racing trying to figure out how she's going to play this, if I'm supposed to make a move or if she's going to.

And then it occurs to me that maybe she's not trying to make a move at all. Maybe I'm entirely misreading what's going on. She could've invited me in here because we've been hanging out. In a turn of events, the emotional part of me is telling me that there's no way she could actually be interested and the logical part of me is the part that's arguing that she's obviously into me. She wouldn't invite me—her declared airport crush—into arguably one of the only private places in an airport for no reason.

She turns and looks at me, stepping toward me. The bathroom isn't big to begin with, so it's easy for her to close the gap in our physical distance.

"You're being very quiet," she says, her voice low. Her eyes travel over my face, making me hyper aware of the expression I most likely have on right now. I don't know what it's communicating to her, but I'm sure it's something entirely unflattering—that I'm nervous, most likely.

"Yeah," I say, because I'm an expert at flirting and know how to effortlessly woo a woman.

"Do you want to help me take my shirt off?"

The pull I feel toward her is like nothing I've ever experienced before. She looks at me through her lashes, just the tiniest bit shorter than me.

I nod before I can find the words, my body responding before my brain. "Yes," I say. She steps even closer to me and I reach out for her, my fingers finding the hem of her shirt.

I take my time, pressing my hands flat to her side. My thumbs find the hem of her shirt and I slowly slide up. When my skin brushes against her skin, I feel her stomach tighten slightly as her body responds to me. Her chest rises and falls more rapidly now.

I keep inching her shirt up, moving past her stomach and toward her ribs. When I'm just nearly cupping her breasts, I move my thumbs to caress her nipples. They're already hard under my touch and she lets out a small breath at the sensation. I feel a rush between my legs and the desire to pick up the pace, to not take our time more than we have to. We don't exactly have all the time in the world here; in fact, we probably don't have much more time at all.

But if this is all I'll ever get of Emmy, I want to relish in every single second of it.

I drop down in front of her and kiss the exposed part of her stomach, looking up at her to see her reaction. Without hesitation, she weaves her fingers through my hair, looking down at me with a needy expression. She wants more from me.

I'm desperate to rip her clothes off and taste her. I want my face between her thighs and to hear her calling my name, moaning it out breathlessly as she cums. I want to feel how wet she can get.

I press my lips to her stomach in a slightly lower spot, working my way down toward her waistband. My hands gently grip her waist, keeping her close to me.

Everything completely melts away. We're not in an airport

anymore and definitely not in an airport bathroom. It doesn't matter where we are. All that matters is that it's me and Emmy and nothing will take this moment from us.

Using my pointer finger, I pull down her waistband just the tiniest bit, kissing skin that's typically hidden from the world. Emmy shudders, letting out at a quiet moan from deep within her. She grips at my hair, holding tight near my scalp.

I smile a little bit. God, that is the most incredible sound in the world followed by the best feeling in the world. It makes me somehow want her even more, something I didn't think was possible.

Realizing the attraction is mutual makes it much easier to lean into the moment. My nerves begin melting away, making me more certain every passing second. It's obvious at this point that she's putty in my hands and doesn't mind it that way; she can flirt a big game, but I'm getting the sense she doesn't mind someone else taking charge.

I pull away and move back up so we're standing face-to-face again. I move my hands around her waist, pulling her in close. We naturally gravitate toward each other, our noses brushing and our lips hovering just a breath apart. I brush her hair out of her face and caress my thumb against her cheek.

When our lips finally touch, I feel my brain chemistry change. I feel every part of me get rewired, recalibrating to understand what genuine desire is. I know in this moment that I've never experienced anything like it before. No amount of flirting at bars can match whatever kind of magic actual attraction is. It makes sense that the person I've had the most fun flirting with of anyone I've met is also the person I'd be the most attracted to of anyone. It's the most intense, most incredible high I've ever experienced.

Her lips are just as soft as I imagined they'd be. She melts into the kiss like she's been waiting for years and not just a few hours. It flows instantly, the two of us exactly on the same wavelength. She wraps her arms around my neck, pressing her bodies together. I slide my hands up her back, feeling every inch of her. When I move back down, I cup her ass, thinking about how easy it would be to just fuck her right here. She rocks her hips against me and I move her hair out of the way so I can kiss her neck.

"Oh, *Harper*," she exhales and I bring her even closer. My hands roam freely over her exposed back and stomach before finally finding her shirt again. I pull her shirt over her head and hold it in my hands, not wanting to let it touch the airport bathroom floor.

With our kiss temporarily broken, we hold each other's gaze. We stay only a slight distance apart, my eyes dancing between her eyes and her partially gaped lips. I brush my thumb over her lips and she kisses the tip.

My eyes travel downwards, taking in her bare chest. Her breasts are perfect—perky, inviting. Her nipples are hard risen mounds I want to run my tongue over.

"Fuck," I say with my free hand, the one not gripping her wet shirt, still on her torso.

I bring my eyes back up to her and we move toward each other to kiss again. But just as our lips are about to brush again, there's a knock at the door. The handle rattles and I pray I'd remembered to lock it in my daze while I was walking in.

Fortunately, the handle holds—the door *is* locked. They knock again.

"We should…" Emmy says at the same time I say, "I think…"

We both nod, not needing to finish our sentence. It feels impossible to move away from her. She also hesitates, her arms still over my shoulders and her fingers toying with my hair.

Another knock at the door finally breaks us apart. I hand off her wet t-shirt.

"Thank you," she says. She looks at it and looks at her suit-case. "I don't know what to do with this."

"Let me hold it for now. You can worry about getting dressed first," I offer and I gently take it from her hands. She pulls on her new shirt from her suitcase and quickly shuts it, zipping up her bag. I fold her shirt in my hands, entirely too enamored by her to find the wet material uncomfortable to hold.

Emmy's back is to me as she pulls her new shirt over her head. I watch the material glide down her bare back and all I can think about is how soft her skin is. I'm already hopelessly addicted, fighting the urge to touch her anywhere I can.

She pulls her hair out from under the hem of her shirt and turns back toward me to see if I'm ready. I step toward her and kiss her again, unsure of if the spell will be broken once we leave. I'm not sure how many more opportunities we'll have to be alone—if any at all. And I don't want to be presumptuous about how willing she is to be seen kissing me around the airport. I'd rather take advantage now.

And it doesn't seem like Emmy minds it, either. She leans into it, taking her hands off of the handle of her suitcase and putting them on either side of my face.

"I wish you could feel how wet I am," she whispers and kisses me again.

She manages to leave me completely speechless. She heads toward the bathroom door and pulls it open. It's not until she's stepping outside that I remember that I have the ability to walk and that I also have to leave.

When we get outside, whoever it was that was knocking on the door isn't even outside anymore. It seems like they probably gave up and went to find the next family restroom they could get to. Part of me wants to yank Emmy right back into the bathroom and jump back into what we'd started, but I have just enough self control to resist.

But not enough self control to resist thinking about what I would've done to her if we'd had more time. And maybe if we hadn't been in an airport bathroom.

Her words will be permanently ingrained in my memory. *I wish you could feel how wet I am.* They keep replaying over and over as I watch Emmy walk just a few steps ahead of me. When she glances back over her shoulder to make sure I'm following, I nearly fall to my knees. The moment plays out almost in slow motion—the way her hair moves, the small smile at her lips when she sees me. She smiles at me like we're sharing a secret. And in some ways, we are. No one else here knows what we just did, what we're both so obviously thinking about.

I watch the way her hips sway, the way her hair moves. I feel an unreasonable sense of possessiveness over her; I want everyone to know that she's with me. I've never been someone who's been particularly territorial but Emmy and I have the kind of unfinished business I don't want anyone to attempt to interrupt.

I follow her without question and without hesitation. We don't have anywhere we need to be in particular with our flight now canceled. It's just us and the airport and the thousands of people attempting to leave before the snow gets too high for people to safely get out.

Around the airport, I see people settling in just like we're about to. There are people laying out in seats, hoods pulled over their eyes. Some have pillows or are using their sweatshirts to get comfortable. Despite the uncertainty and obvious annoyance radiating from everyone in the airport, there's also something kind of sweet about some of the interactions. There are kids, completely oblivious to how stressed their parents are. Friends laughing and sharing snacks. People Face-Timing each other.

I feel another tug in my heart at the thought of Hannah's wedding. As fun as this adventure with Emmy has been, I would never have picked a rendezvous like this over my best friend's bachelorette party and wedding. If I had the option to get on a plane and go to her now, I would.

I know I have to call her. Once Emmy and I get settled somewhere, I'll let Hannah know that I won't be leaving but I'm going to do everything I can to get on the first flight out. I'm mostly relieved it's not a super long flight. And I'm also relieved that Hannah has never once been capable of guilt tripping someone. The chillness that radiates from her makes it easier to

"This one is empty," Emmy says. I'm matching her pace now, walking beside her. She leads us over to a gate and beelines to a spot on the floor toward the back.

"Do you ever sit in the actual seats?" I ask.

"I like the floor. I can spread out—and there's usually outlets around," she says and scans the surrounding walls. She moves her rolling overhead bag to the side, out of the way. As she does, her hair falls just the tiniest bit in her face and over her shoulders. The shirt she's wearing now is just as flattering to her frame, braving a tank top despite it being winter in Colorado. I know San Francisco is California but it's not exactly the warmest time of year.

"You packed tank tops for this trip?" I ask.

"I knew I was going to have a run-in with someone hot and wanted to make sure I was wearing only my most flattering clothes," I say and my cheeks flush. I'm embarrassed by how relieved I am that the flirting isn't over even though we left the bathroom.

"Oh, of course. I don't know how I didn't think of that," I say.

Emmy settles onto the floor, her back against the wall. She pulls out a charger from her bag and gets comfortable, plugging her phone in but promptly putting it to the side instead of checking it.

"It's actually just my airport clothes. I usually get pretty sweaty walking around, especially when they have the heat on like this. I like to layer up," she says. "I have warm clothes otherwise. I don't know what I'm going to do when I have to fly back from San Francisco now, though."

"Be sweaty, I guess," I tease and sit down on the floor next to her. I readjust, careful to keep some distance from Emmy even though I'm dying to touch her. The wall is, as can be imagined, very hard against my spine and the floor offers zero cushion. Cold air from the outside radiates through the closed airport windows.

The view from here isn't terrible, though. There's something kind of beautiful about the snow despite the fact it's completely derailed my day. Ant-sized airport employees do the best they can to clear out the snow as it's falling. The sun is beginning to set, casting a warm glow over the partially snow-covered tarmac.

I readjust, hoping that maybe there's a way to get comfortable here. But I'm "I don't know how this is your preference."

Emmy laughs. "It's...cozy."

"For sure," I say, snorting out a laugh.

"It's what we have," she says. And there it is again—*we*. Warmth blooms in my chest at the word. And, unfortunately, so does hope. And I can tell immediately that I'm not going to be able to play it cool. As much as I want to be able to be normal about what Emmy and I got up to in the bathroom, I don't think I can. The haze is gone and reality is starting to sink in. I can already tell I'm going to be thinking about her for a long time to come.

I've been single for long enough and had enough shitty dating experiences to know that hope is one of the scariest feelings to experience while getting to know someone new. Once there's hope, there's something to lose. There's waiting for a text back, overanalyzing conversations, wondering if it's actually going to last or if something is going to change. And something always seems to change. It doesn't matter how things start or how much it seems like we're into each other—things *always* go south.

And as much as I want to be able to jump head first and take that risk and accept that as part of life's beautiful journey, it's scary. It's giving something to someone else, even if it's just mild interest or my time. It's opening up the door to heartbreak, or even just basic disappointment.

I have the basic awareness to know that we just met and no amount of genuine weight can be attached to our relationship so far. Logically, I know this. We're really only one step up from strangers. Maybe barely more than just a one night stand. But I know myself and I know how quickly I can run with even the tiniest amount of interest. With someone like Emmy, a casual *we should get together when you're back in town* will really mean something. It'll hurt if we don't.

Or at least, it'll hurt me. I can't speak for how she would feel.

"I'll be right back," I say and as soon as I stand up, I know I did it with too much urgency. I can see on Emmy's face that she's a little startled.

I feel immediately bad but I'm also suddenly filled with so much anxiety over whatever the hell we're doing that I know I can't sit still. I need to walk it off, need to talk to Hannah. I have to level myself out and get out of his headspace of attaching more value to Emmy and I hanging out than what actually exists.

"Okay," she says and for the first time since I've known her, her easy expression falters. It feels like a knife in my chest to see the way she blinks at me, the way her lips turn down just slightly. She's quick to cover it up, but it's there.

I turn to walk away.

"Wait, Harper—" Emmy says and I turn around to look at her again. "Are you taking your bags?"

"Oh, I…I can just leave them here," I say and consider that might be a really stupid idea. I don't actually know her. But there's nothing really that valuable other than clothes in my overhead bag. I still have my backpack with me—my phone and my wallet are secure.

And, above all else, I'm stupidly trusting. I know who I am and I know that my gut reaction is going to be that the nice, pretty girl with the sweet smile isn't going to steal my shit, even though that's exactly how it would go.

"That's technically against airport rules," Emmy says and I can hear in her tone that she's back to teasing me. There isn't any suggestion that she's worried about why I'm leaving. I respect the boldness. I know if our roles were reversed, I'd be burrowing away and assuming I'd done something horribly embarrassing. My walls would probably start coming up, because they have a tendency to do that when I get even the tiniest whiff that someone might not be interested in me like I am in them.

But there's Emmy—bold and forward and refusing to read between the lines. It looks good on her.

I walk back toward her, pulled in magnetically by the way her lips are turned upwards and the way she's looking at me. I meet her on the ground again, leaning over her legs.

"Against airport rules?" I ask.

She nods, moving forward so the gap between our faces is only a couple of inches. "I'm not supposed to watch a stranger's bag."

"You think of me as a stranger?" I tease back. Our voices have dropped to nearly a whisper and it feels like it's only us in the entire airport. I brush a piece of hair from her face.

"Strangers enough that I don't know for sure you don't have something illegal in your bags."

"Would that be a dealbreaker for you?"

Emmy is quiet for a moment, acting as though she's really thinking about it. "It wouldn't be if it was you."

I can't help but smile a little bit. The most nervous parts of myself are telling me to get it together. They're telling me that these are probably all just lines and that she's this good with everyone and that it doesn't really mean anything. The part of me that's the most afraid of all desperately wants to just ask her right then if she's interested in me, if she sees this actually being something.

This is familiar territory for me. I don't crush easily, but when I do, it's hard and fast and all-consuming. I become someone who wants to know way too soon what's going on and what the other person wants of me. I know it's self-preservation. And the impulse is so strong to just let it all blow up before it can fizzle out organically.

But Emmy is also sitting here in front of me, beautiful and kind. She's here for the moment. And when she's looking at me, it makes it a little easier to quiet the most self destructive and reckless parts of myself.

I lean in, gauging if she wants me to kiss her. She moves closer to me, our lips hovering so close to each other. This feels like something new between us. We're in public; we can't have sex here. We'd be kissing for the sake of kissing, kissing because we want to and don't care if other people see.

Fuck it.

I lean in and kiss her and when she kisses me back, it reminds me of why I'm even freaking out in the first place. Kissing her isn't just a kiss; it's something else entirely. It satisfies something in me that I didn't think could be satisfied. It makes me want to never stop.

She pulls away slowly, like her body is rejecting the decision. "Weren't you going somewhere?"

"I was," I say. "I should go call Hannah."

She nods, weaving her hand through mine. It occurs to me that it's the first time that we've held hands and if it's a method to keep me with her longer, it's working. "Okay. Don't be gone too long," she says.

I chuckle. "Okay," I say.

We keep our eyes fixed on each other for a beat and I consider kissing her again. But I know if I do, I'll never get up and I'll never call Hannah and I'll keep getting myself into deeper and deeper shit.

I finally separate myself from Emmy and stand up, walking off. I'm embarrassed by how I immediately want to go back to her and how I feel like I should be spending every second I can with her.

I walk a good distance away—down the hallway and to a completely different terminal—so I won't risk Emmy hearing anything. I find an empty gate and throw myself into the furthest seat away from people walking by, sitting right near a window. I drop my backpack on the floor at my feet and dial Hannah's number.

The second the phone call clicks through to her, I let it out.

"Hannah, I'm so fucked," I say.

chapter five

"WHAT HAPPENED?" Hannah asks. I can hear voices around her and then the sound of her walking. It's easy for me to picture her in her beautiful apartment, probably leaving the living room to go into her bedroom. When the door shuts behind her, I know she's ready to gossip.

"Sorry, I didn't mean to interrupt—are you doing wedding prep?" I ask. Not only am I stuck in the airport and unable to get to her for one of the most important days of her life, I'm now pulling her away from the last wedding prep that I should be helping her with. I check the time and sure enough, I should've been with her by now.

"No, it's okay. I always have time for you," she says. "I saw the flight was canceled."

"Right, you have the text updates on," I say.

"Are you okay? Are you going home until the next flight is announced?"

"I think I'm going to brave it here," I say. My mind flashes to Emmy. I know she's a major reason why I'm willing to stick it out and not even really try to go home, but she's not necessarily the *only* reason. "I don't want to pay for collectively, like, four Ubers just trying to get in and out of the airport. I'm also hoping that maybe if I stay close I can get on a flight sooner."

"You'd rather sleep on the airport floor than just go home?" she asks. I can hear her expression in her voice, the tender look on her face whenever someone does something nice for her. She always earnestly presses her hand to her chest like she's a touched grandma and furrows her brow in such a specific way.

Thinking about it makes me sad. It's been a long time since we've been physically in the same place. Long distance friendship has proven to not be impossible. In fact, there have been a lot of perks—I love having an excuse to come see her, and she'll fly out to see me for long weekends when she can. It doesn't matter how long we've been apart; we always come right back together, clicking as though we never spent any time apart.

But now that we're on the phone and I'm thinking about how I should be there with her, I'm sad about it. Since moving away from home and from the, frankly, really perfect, story-book life I had in college, I've become the master at pushing down my feelings. I focus on all of the positives—my friends and I are all growing up, we're all independent, we're all still very much in touch and still all care about each other. We do everything we can to see each other when we can.

But now that time with Hannah has been put on the table, having it suddenly taken away really sucks. Especially when we're supposed to be getting together for something so important.

My eyes well up with tears and I'm embarrassed even though I know people cry in airports all the time for all different reasons. I turn my head away from the people walking by and look out the window instead.

"I'd like to eventually make it for your wedding extrava-ganza," I say, hoping the humor comes through more so than the sadness. I don't want Hannah to worry. But asking her not to worry is like asking water not to be wet.

"Oh, it'll be okay, Harper. Really," she says gently. "You're not the only person facing delays coming in. I'm glad so many people decided to fly in early. You teased me about wanting to have a whole long weekend itinerary but it looks like it has its benefits. The storm will blow through so soon and then you'll be here and it'll be fine."

I nod, taking a deep breath. "You're right," I say, not because I know for sure—I haven't checked the forecast in a few hours—but because Hannah seems so confident. It's one of my favorite things about her; she knows how to regulate me. She does a better job at it than my own family ever has.

"Now, will you tell me what's *really* going on? Because I know you're a dedicated friend, but the distress in your voice cannot possibly be related to the wedding."

I blush. "I hate that you know me so well."

"Is it that girl from Hinge? Is she back?"

"Oh, which one? The one who kept trying to booty call me even though we'd never met before or the one who ghosted after we made plans to hangout?"

Hannah snorts out a laugh. "I'm hoping neither of them."

I take a deep breath. The confidence I'd felt dialing her up is waning now and I'm nervous to admit everything out loud. Saying anything at all about Emmy to someone who isn't her makes all of this feel suddenly very real. "Yeah," I say, because my heart is beating so fast that it's rendered my brain useless.

"Wait, did you meet someone?" she asks. I nearly laugh; she's always known me too well to let me get away with anything. There's a beat of no more than half a second before she gasps. "Oh my god, you totally did. Who is it?"

"It's so scary to me how well you know me," I say. "You didn't even give me the chance to confirm yes or no."

"The only time you're *ever* certain you're fucked is when

you have a crush on someone," Hannah says. "Is this someone you met at the airport? You totally have a crush on someone from the airport. That is *so* romantic comedy coded."

"It's not a *crush*—"

"You think someone is cute. Whatever. Semantics. All that matters is you're interested in someone," she says. "Did you meet at the airport? What's their name? Airport crush or real crush?"

"I think maybe a real crush," I say. "We've been...talking."

"Okay, that's promising. Some would say that's the ideal outcome of having a crush."

"There's also been maybe...more than talking."

Hannah shrieks so loudly that I have to pull my phone away from my ear. "You're kidding! *Yes*! This is the best wedding present you could ever give me! Where did you guys kiss? Did you sneak away somewhere in the airport? That is so hot. It's like the mile-high club but somehow even hotter because it's so hard to be alone anywhere in an actual airport."

"Okay, wait—I haven't been single for *that* long. Give me some credit," I say.

"But it's been *so* long since you've come to me with a crush. You've gone on so many random dates and talked about so many random people from dating apps. This is something actually real. I love this."

"Actually real feels like an overstatement. We don't really know each other, we only met a couple of hours ago."

"And you guys have been hanging out this whole time?"

"Basically. We met when we were waiting in line to talk to customer service."

"I'm over the moon, personally," she says. "See, meeting someone in person isn't entirely impossible! Meet cutes are all around!"

"Let's not get too far ahead of ourselves."

"What's their name?"

I take a deep breath. We're actually getting into it now. Hannah's enthusiasm is rubbing off on me but it's also making me more nervous. It feels like the classic crush curse—the second you start to think something is happening, the second you tell your friends, it all crashes and burns.

"Emmy," I say. "She's...great, Hannah. I think you'd really like her. She's kind. And she's a grad student. And she's..." I trail off, thinking back to our time in the bathroom together. The sound of her softly panting, the needy little moans she let out. The way my entire body seems to practically vibrate with need whenever I'm around her.

"This is a huge day," Hannah says, oblivious to the fact that my mind had gone somewhere else entirely for a moment. She pauses. "Wait, okay so what kind of more than talking are you guys getting up to at the airport?"

"We might've found a single-occupant bathroom," I say.

Hannah squeals so loudly again that I have to move my phone away from my ear again. "That is so hot."

"I know, she's...I don't know. She's amazing. It's stupid."

"It's not stupid. I think gut feeling can say a lot," she says. "Think about the number of people you've been out with who you've felt absolutely nothing for after a date."

"That's fair," I say. She's right—there have been people I've gone out with who I think I'll really like who end up doing nothing for me. It can be any combination of things, usually not even related to physical attraction. It'll be the way they communicate, their sense of humor, their approach to flirting. There will just be no chemistry or a complete lack of compatibility. It makes sense why I'd feel so caught off guard and overwhelmed by everything with Emmy; it's rare to find someone you like more as you get to know them.

"Is she from the area?"

"Yeah, she is. She was supposed to be on my flight to San Francisco—she's going out there for an academic conference."

"Okay, a hot nerd," she says. "And even more fun than that—hot nerd who isn't afraid to get down to business in an airport. I like her already."

"You don't need to like her, I don't think it'll be going past this," I say, not wanting to get too far ahead of myself. The thought of Emmy meeting Hannah is a lot for me. I can already see them hitting it off, gossiping and laughing together like they've been friends for forever. Thinking about it makes me want it and I can't afford to want something like that.

"What's with the negativity?" Hannah asks. "Has there been any mention of you guys hanging out again? I mean, if you're both from there, it seems stupid to not just continue to see each other. It's not like you're in Before Sunrise. You're only going to be, like, driving distance apart."

"Yeah, but it's...more complex than that. I don't know if she wants to hangout past this. It might just be a fun fling for her. She might not be looking for anything."

"Have you asked her?"

I can already tell where this is going. "No."

"Then why are you assuming she's not also genuinely into you?" Hannah asks.

There it is.

I take a deep breath. That's always been Hannah's favorite question. Ever since we met freshman year and I came out to her in the process of admitting I had a debilitating crush on our RA—it was not mutual—Hannah has reliably kept me in check. She'll call out my anxiety and tell me when I'm over-thinking something. She'll push me to just send the text, even if it's scary and we both know it probably won't end well. But she also knows when to pull back. She'll take my phone from me when she's worried I might drunk text someone I shouldn't, and talks me down whenever I begin to get too delusional over a crush both of us knows isn't going anywhere.

She is, in so many ways, such a good friend. But she's also

the most intense friend I have when it comes to getting my shit together. There's no one I trust more and no one I fear more in equal measure.

"I don't want to ask," I say.

"You don't want to ruin what you have," she says, filling in the blanks.

I nod as if she can see me. "I'm worried about asking too soon. But I'm also worried about asking too late and missing the window completely. Or misreading some kind of signal."

"I mean, I really do believe there's nothing some communication can't fix, so long as both people are ready to communicate," she says. "I do believe you can say the wrong thing to the right person and hurt one or both of your feelings, but if they really like you, they'll stick it out with you. If you move too fast or too slow, she'll probably understand. She'll want to work with you on it if she likes you too. Just don't wait, like, months to follow-up with her if she gives you her number—even I would tell her to tell you to fuck off."

"Yeah," I say, my heart pounding with nerves. All sorts of new anxieties swirl within me. Maybe it's not Emmy that I have to worry about. Maybe I'm the one who's moving too quickly. I'm just looking for someone and Emmy happens to fit the criteria of being exciting enough and fun enough. Maybe I won't actually want it to be something more beyond this.

"I can practically hear you spiraling out," Hannah says, interrupting my spiraling out.

"I'm not," I lie. A silent beat passes between us. "Okay, maybe a little. I'm just *nervous*. It all feels so intense. But it also feels so stupid. Like, I know it's not really that serious. But I also think it's, like, the most serious thing in the world."

"Having a crush...what a high," Hannah teases, but I can hear the compassion in her voice. Before meeting Alexander, Hannah had been put through the ringer. She's endlessly kind, which seemed to only ever attract the worst people I've ever met. It would be asshole after asshole in college. Part of it wasn't even them; Hannah owns up to the fact that her taste has always been pretty garbage and she knows she should've had the sense to have chosen better.

Crushes for her—just like for me—had mostly been a humiliation ritual. But then she met Alexander and it all changed and now she's wildly happy. The big difference between us presently is that they *were*, past tense, a humiliation ritual for Hannah; they still are for me.

"I didn't ask for this," I groan pathetically, leaning into my palms.

"I actually think you did," she said. "Do you want me to pull up the texts of you begging for something exciting to happen in your dating life?"

"No, wait—"

"Wait, I literally have one you sent, like, six texts ago. *I think I'm going to redownload Hinge. I take back what I said about dating, I'm lonely—*"

"Oh no, I think our call is dropping. Oh no, I'm losing you," I say, not needing the reminder that Hannah is totally right. As much as I'll protest against a crush, I'm always a tiny bit relieved when I have one. It adds a little something special to life. It gives us purpose in a very specific way. As much as I love my friends and my family, the type of love that comes from romantic connection is unlike anything else.

"And here's another: *I don't think I'm ever meant to actually find love.* I love that. You sent that at, like, ten a.m. on a Tuesday."

"*Nooo*," I moan, mortified. "You win. Point proven. Stop harassing me."

Hannah cackles on the other end. "I say go for it with her. Don't be a coward. Let it play out how it may."

"But that's so scary," I whine.

"Let it be scary. It was scary for me when I first started seeing Alexander."

"No it wasn't. He's been obsessed with you since the day you met and he's never once made you doubt his feelings for you."

"Okay fair," she says and then goes quiet for a second. "*But* that didn't mean I'm not still afraid of my own feelings for him at times. And I mean, allowing someone the possibility of hurting you will always be scary no matter what. Alexander has been incredible but he's also human. He's hurt my feelings before. I'm very aware of how it would devastate me if he suddenly up and left, even though I know in my heart he'd never do something like that."

I sigh a little bit. "I don't really believe either of you have ever had any doubts in your relationship but I appreciate the support."

"Not doubts—just vulnerability. What you're feeling right now is about being nervous she might not feel the same. It's *normal*. It's *fine*. You just have to ride it out. Keep taking it one step at a time. Enjoy it while you have it," she says. "I know it's impossible for you to get yourself out of your head, but give it a chance. Go all in with her and have your beautiful one night together if that's all this will be. Ask her for her number if you want it. The worst that happens is all of this stops tomorrow and then you just have to continue on with business as usual without her. The world won't stop spinning."

I let her words sink in. I'm desperate to lean into them, wanting to be carefree and fun. I want to embrace the version of Hannah that came before Alexander. She's always been the same—confident, kind, warm. People flock to her. She floated through bars effortlessly, people offering to buy her drinks left and right either with romantic intention or just because she's cool as fuck. In college, I watched her recover from heartbreak after heartbreak in record time, never letting it slow her down. She never lets herself get worked up because she always knows someone else will come along eventually. And when someone wasn't there, she was still having the time of her life because being single is a lot less scary when you earnestly believe a life partner is out there.

"Go kiss her again," Hannah says. "I think you'll feel a lot better actually with her than just spiraling out on the phone with me."

"Okay, okay," I say, knowing she's right. Part of me is excited to run off to Emmy again, wanting to see what we'll say and how things will go and what's going to happen next. But another part of me is nervous to have to jump right back in. The anticipation is killer; I know that's what's making my palms slick with sweat. The meanest part of my brain is thinking up all kinds of scenarios, including one where she actually does disappear with all of my stuff.

"Keep me updated on flights. The bachelorette isn't until tomorrow evening, so you have a little leeway."

"I'm sad I'm missing your family dinner," I say. That's the first thing on the itinerary—Hannah is getting her immediate family, which is her sisters, her dad, her mom and me as a honorary sibling together for a dinner. Nearly everyone in Hannah's family moved somewhere away from home, so it's hard to get everyone into the same place. I haven't seen some of her sisters in person in almost five years, which is hard to believe considering how much time I spent with them growing up. I'd been looking forward to catching up with them in a setting slightly more intimate than a bachelorette party and the wedding as a whole.

"It'll be okay. They're all going to the rehearsal dinner so any catching up you don't do over shots at my bach can be done there."

"Not the threat of shots."

"Not a threat—a *promise*," Hannah teases. "But okay, seriously. Even if you're stalling because you're nervous, I actually do have to go because we're finishing some of the centerpieces before heading off to dinner."

"Alright," I say, realizing that this is really it and I'm going to have to go back to Emmy now. I can't keep using Hannah as a way of putting this off.

"I love you. Stay warm," she says. "And send updates, I'm dying to know how this all ends up going."

"If you don't hear anything, just assume it didn't go well."

"Or I'll assume you're too busy fooling around in bathrooms to answer my texts."

"Okay, I'm hanging up now," I say as Hannah laughs.

We end the call and I drop my phone in my lap, sighing a little bit. I feel better having spoken to Hannah, but even she can't completely ease my anxiety. She's right that the only thing that will help is going back to Emmy and leaning into it.

Despite how cowardly I'm feeling, there is also a part of me that's excited by all of this. It's hard *not* to just lean in and say fuck it to any consequences. Maybe I'll end up totally devastated by all of this, maybe I'll spend the next month or two or three recovering from one perfect night with a stranger. But that is more exciting than not doing it at all.

I stand up and head back toward Emmy in the next terminal over. I can't distinguish what I'm feeling; it's something new entirely to me. Since I tend to avoid casual—my relationships are all or nothing, all love or only sex—I don't really know what to do in this situation. It feels like dangerous territory continuing to play into a crush that might not go anywhere. I've managed to completely sabotage most of my crushes. My best success rate is landing one-night stands, casual in a completely different way. They're easy; this is not.

It isn't until I see Emmy that my brain seems to actually quiet down. I see her from a distance as I'm approaching the gate, her eyes fixed on her phone. She's in the same exact spot, our bags next to her. She looks completely at ease.

She looks up, eyes scanning the room. When she realizes it's me who's looking at her, her face breaks out into an easy smile. My lips naturally turn upward in response.

I keep walking toward her, everything from earlier melting away. Now that she's in front of me, all I want is to be next to her.

As I get closer, she puts her phone down. I drop down to the floor, leaning toward her. We kiss effortlessly, like we've been doing it for years. It's so organic that I don't even question how bold it is for me to do something like that. When it comes to a crush, to the possibility of genuine rejection, I never kiss first.

I kiss her again, letting it deepen. I let desire course wildly through me without fighting against the feeling or getting nervous about it. I force myself to be completely in the moment and entirely wrapped up in her. It's just like I've been telling myself—if I only get one night with her, I might as well make the most of it.

Her hands find my face, her touch gentle. Her hands are the tiniest bit cold and I'm surprised by how intense my desire is to warm them.

"Hi," she says when we finally break apart.

"Hi," I say.

chapter six

"YOU'RE BACK," she says.

"I had to come get my stuff eventually," I say. We stay facing each other as I sit back, my arm propped up over Emmy's legs. I'll move so my back is up against the wall again eventually but for now, I'm okay with just looking at her.

"Right, of course," she says. "Always happy to watch your things for you and then send you on your merry way."

"Did you steal anything from my bag?" I tease.

"You'll just have to wait and see," she says. She laces our hands together, taking my free one into her lap. I caress my thumb over her hand and try to offer at least some warmth. With the sun quickly going down, the temperature is dropping fast. It's made our little nest near the windows a lot less cozy and a lot draftier than before.

"Do you need a sweatshirt?" I ask, aware of Emmy's bare shoulders. My eyes trail down to the modest scoop over her cleavage and the way her nipples press against the material. I'm brought right back to us in the bathroom together, the switch inside of me flipping almost instantly. There's no need for a warm up when Emmy just casually looks like that.

But as much as I don't mind getting to see so much of her, I can only imagine she's freezing.

"Are you offering me one of yours?" she asks.

"No, I'm just asking."

She smiles a little bit, catching my dry joke. "If you have a spare one."

I take my overhead bag by the handle and lay it down flat, unzipping it and popping it open. I can't remember how I packed it—all I know is that it's not nearly as neat as how Emmy organizes hers. Inside is pretty much all wedding stuff that I either just bought or almost never wear—black suit pants, nice shirts, my nicest pair of formal shoes. There's no real system to it, so I have to dig through all of my things in order to find what I'm looking for.

"This is a Harper classic," I say and hand off a pullover sweatshirt that's nothing more than a plain blue sweatshirt with the name of my high school across the front. It's old and faded but so worn in that it feels like wearing the world's softest blanket. I should maybe be more precious about it, but Emmy gives me the impression that she's not going anywhere. I trust her to wear it.

And anyway, I've never been the kind of person to say no to a hot girl wearing my clothes.

"*Ooh*," Emmy says with the appropriate amount of enthusiasm, raising her eyebrows at me. Her full lips form a perfect O. She takes the sweatshirt from my hands and as soon as she touches it, her playful expression drops into something I can tell is more genuine. "Oh, wow. This actually is nice."

I laugh. "No, I know. It doesn't look like much but I really like it."

"Yeah, the paint stains really add a little...something."

"My favorite detail is that the lettering is falling off, personally," I say. The yellow iron-on material is cracked and chipping away. Looking at it now so plainly out in the open and out of the context of my bedroom is making me realize just how rough it looks.

But Emmy is handling it like it's the most precious thing she's ever touched, gingerly pulling it over her head and pulling her hair out from the neckline.

Seeing her in it—the sweatshirt that's too big for me so it's definitely too big for her—makes my heart go into double-time. My breath suddenly feels shallow. It's so wildly intimate, her wearing my clothes. She's not the first person, and she's not even the first person who's not a girlfriend. There have been one night stands who've needed t-shirts, failed 'situation-ships' that borrowed my jackets when it got chilly during a night out.

But it's different with Emmy.

She looks at me with her giant brown eyes and smiles a little bit. I blush, embarrassed to be so plainly staring at her.

"I'm sorry it doesn't match," I say. To fit with the rest of her generally tailored and put-together demeanor, her outfit is perfectly coordinated. It's in a way that looks organic and casual, but I'm getting the sense that she's someone who's careful about the way she carries herself. There's nothing sloppy about her. I don't know her well, but seeing her in a sweatshirt with paint streaked on it is still kind of funny to me.

It makes me wonder what her apartment looks like, what her car looks like. I wonder if everything in her life is just as organized as her suitcase and as coordinated as her clothing, or if she's just a really prepared traveler.

"It's perfect," she says. She pulls her hands inside the arms of the sweatshirt, curling up inside. I zip up my bag again and join her with my back against the wall. When her body starts leaning toward mine, I don't fight against it. She lets her knees fall partially into my lap, her head hovering just barely near my shoulder. It feels strangely natural even though we don't really know each other.

I've never been someone who's been open to casual intimacy in that way with someone I'm not seeing. Sex tends to be one thing, but the idea of someone in my bed beyond the act, someone sleeping over, someone just physically being close to me, isn't something I'm usually open to unless I'm into them.

And with Emmy, it feels like I physically can't get enough. I find myself wanting her to be even closer.

"So, what do we do now?" she asks, looking out to where people are walking around the airport. There's a sense of restlessness; it's obvious who has decided to just commit to staying here versus who is getting a hotel. And just like with us, it seems like the reality of sleeping on the floor and being stuck in the airport for probably another twelve hours at least is setting in.

"I don't know, actually. I've never done this before," I say. And then think about it. "Should we see if the fire pits are open? I'm sure they're packed if they are but might be worth a shot. We can try laying out your shirt too and see if it'll dry."

"You just hate sitting on the floor."

"I'm sure I'm in the minority there. Laying on the floor when you need it is one thing, but sitting on the floor is a completely different story. Much less comfortable. Not nearly as good for the back."

"It's part of the airport experience. I would never sit on the floor anywhere else, I swear."

"You mean you don't go to a restaurant and ask to sit on the floor? Odd."

Emmy snorts out a laugh. "Okay, let's go check out these fire pits or whatever."

"Fire pits or *whatever*?" I echo. "You say that as if they're not an amazing perk of this airport."

"I've never seen them before. I usually try to get in and out of the airport as quickly as possible."

"*What*?" I ask. "The airport is part of the experience!

There's aimless wandering. People watching. Food court fast food and tiny plastic containers of grapes that cost twelve dollars. It's perfect. It doesn't get any better than this."

"There's no way you actually like the airport. No one likes the airport."

"I love it here," I say. "Every trip I take, I'll come early just to wander around." I pause for a second. "Part of it might have to do with extreme anxiety around being late and missing my flight. But at least I channel it in a healthy way."

"Yeah, you sound really sane—"

"Okay, alright." I laugh.

Emmy gets up and brushes off her leggings. "Okay, let's see it. Let's do the airport. I'll let you be the guide since you love it here so much."

"You're so on."

"An adventure."

My lips turn up in a smile. "An adventure."

We gather our things and start heading off in the general direction of the fire pits. I'm not confident in my navigation skills—I spend time in the airport but not so much time that I have the entire floor plan memorized—but I try not to let that on to Emmy. I don't think she'd earnestly make fun of me for shitty navigation abilities and I'm usually not prone to embarrassment, but something about getting lost with a hot girl does not feel sexy.

We keep up pace with each other, weaving between people walking with little to no urgency, something I never understood in the airport.

"Do you travel much?" Emmy asks while we walk.

"Some," I say. "Because I don't live near my parents, I try to see them when I can. We do a lot of meeting in the middle or picking somewhere that isn't home. Mostly domestic travel. But I did study abroad in France for a semester."

"How old?"

"Junior year. It was cool. I don't really get homesick so it was genuinely really fun. It made me realize there's no reason for me to stay close to home when I start looking for work," I say. I turn to look at her. "What about you?"

Her fingers find mine, casually intertwining them. My breath catches at the sudden casual contact and the feeling of her skin. I hope it isn't obvious, but I know it almost definitely is. I feel like I'm showing all of my thoughts so apparently on my face.

"I also studied abroad. I was in Italy, though," she says. "Only for a few weeks. It wasn't a full semester. I, unfortunately, did get homesick so it was hard for me. I spent basically my entire freshman year trying to be brave about it but being so incredibly lonely and lost. I thought Italy might help put things into perspective but it ended up being so hard. I'm hoping to go back eventually to kind of...reclaim it, I think. I haven't left the country since—mostly as a money issue, not a fear issue."

"It's surprising to me you get homesick." As we're walking, I keep my eyes peeled for where we're supposed to go. I'm trying to pay as close attention as I can to what Emmy is saying, but I also am trying *really* hard to not get us totally turned around out here.

"Yeah? Because I give off such a tough girl, independent energy?" she teases lightly.

"You do come across as really independent. But you were talking about how excited you were to leave home and everything."

"It turns out being excited to leave home is a totally different thing from actually leaving home," Emmy says with a small smile. "I spent a lot of time talking to my therapist about it. I've gotten a lot better now. It feels like over time, it's become easier and easier for me to be away from home. I still miss it sometimes, but it's in such specific ways. I'll miss, like,

Sunday mornings on my parents' couch. Taking walks around my neighborhood. My sister doing my makeup. The library I grew up going to." She shrugs. "I know deep down my hometown isn't the right fit for me, but it's kind of like wanting to go back to a high school ex or something. It just feels...familiar. It's so much safer to go back than it is to go forward."

"Yeah, I get that," I say, even though I don't really. It's been one of my biggest issues through life; I seem to actively fight against nostalgia every step of the way.

Emmy looks at me, tilting her head up to look at me. Her eyes dance over my face like she's studying me. "I don't know if you do," she says. Her tone isn't accusatory; it's sweet, instead. It makes me think she really actually sees me. She can cut straight through my attempt at bullshit.

"This way," I say, pointing ahead. I'm starting to recognize this part of the airport and I'm pretty sure the fire pits are somewhere around here. "But no, you're right," I admit. "I don't really get it. It probably comes back to my parents in some way, since they're not really nostalgic people either. There's a lot of thought about the present, which is beautiful. But in exchange, I think I've forgotten how to reminisce and be grateful for the things that I've experienced in the past. I'm able to move so far ahead without looking back, but then it means I'm quick to just move into the next chapter without thinking about it."

Eventually, I spot the fire pits on the outside deck area. It's crowded but not nearly as crowded as I imagined it would be, probably because it's so cold out here. A little bit of snow has fallen onto the patio.

Emmy beelines to an open seat and puts her stuff to the side. She gestures for me to sit on the couch and I sit down. I sit with the intent of creating a reasonable distance between us, but Emmy immediately closes it. I have to turn my head away from her for a moment so I don't risk her seeing the cheesy smile spreading across my face.

We're both quiet for a moment, enjoying the heat of the fire as we sit. "This is really nice. I had no idea these were here," Emmy says. She curls up into me. "Cold, though."

"Yeah, it's a great addition. Every airport in a city prone to snow should have these," I say. I take her shirt that I've been committed to holding and lay it out over the arm of the couch. I'm not sure it's hot enough out here to really do anything, but it's worth a shot.

"Thank you," she says. "That's really nice of you."

"Yeah, of course," I say, surprised by how surprised she sounds. "I'm the one who spilled something on you. I want to at least try to find a solution."

She wraps her arm around mine, leaning against my shoulder. "What are you like when you're dating?"

I let out a surprised laugh. "What's the segue?"

"The ability to just move onto the next thing. Is that for everything?"

The answer completely takes me off guard. It takes me a second to realize she's referring back to our earlier conversation before we got sidetracked by the fire pits. My face blushes hot and a spark courses through me at what I'm pretty sure she's suggesting. It doesn't seem like a question she's asking just for the sake of asking it. It seems like the kind of question someone wouldn't ask unless they have a specific goal in mind —especially considering she's bringing the topic up herself. Clearly, what I'd said had made an impact.

I don't want to go too far ahead and assume it means anything, but I can already feel myself sprinting with it. In a flash, I see so much—the two of us texting through our time in San Francisco, Emmy coming to visit my apartment, making space in my calendar to drive and see her. Even if it's not forever, it's so easy to imagine us doing it in the immediate future.

And most surprising of all is that the thought doesn't scare me. After being single for so long, there are times when I question how capable I am of developing feeling this strong and knowing when I've met someone I like. I've had many long nights of wondering if I'm looking in the wrong places and if I should've just given that person from a few months ago more of a chance.

But being here with Emmy is making me realize that I've always been capable of knowing when I like someone. The ability has always been there, just hiding under the surface and waiting for an excuse to come back up.

I freeze, thinking through how I want to answer her question. I want to be careful about it, not immediately jumping in and scaring her off with too much intensity. But I also don't want to give her the kind of answer that makes her think I don't care about her and that I'm some kind of player who fucks and dumps like it's no big deal.

"It's situational," I say. I trace my thumb over her hand. "It depends on how emotionally ready I am to let go of something. I've held onto the hurt over some crushes longer than I've held onto some breakups. I don't know what the pattern is, if there is any." I look over at her. "What about you?"

She smiles a little bit. "Probably my biggest red flag is how hard it is for me to get over anything that's ever happened to me. But my boundaries are pretty good, so it's never really bitten me. The people I've dated have historically been pretty nice."

"Ouch—*pretty nice*? If I had an ex whose primary description of me was that I was pretty nice, I would never recover."

She laughs. "I think they'd probably say the same thing about me. Lots of incredibly...neutral relationships. Nice people being nice to each other. But it lacked *passion*."

"Sometimes passion isn't all it's cracked up to be," I say. "It's unfortunately very easy to mistake passion for someone who just isn't a good fit for you."

Emmy's eyes widen with curiosity. "I *know* there's a story there and you have to tell me."

"It's not worth explaining," I say, waving my hand. "Nothing exciting. It's just the wrong thing with the wrong person. A willingness to get myself into things just to see what'll happen and then realizing it actually sucks and it's not worth the story. I'd rather experience something level at this point. Someone who's just, like, nice to me and consistent."

"That is such a hot person problem to have," she teases.

I laugh, my face burning hot. "What could that possibly mean?"

"You have enough options to feel like you can date for fun and for the stories rather than needing to take it seriously. You know someone else will always come along," she says. "I admire it, honestly."

"And you expect me to believe you don't have people lining up to go out with you? What about your hot person dating problems?" I say.

She leans further into my lap, putting her hand on my leg as she laughs. "That is not true. Don't try to flatter me like that."

"I mean, look at you," I say, the joking tone suddenly disappearing from my voice and instead being replaced with something significantly more genuine. The air between us changes in an instant. I don't mean for it to happen, but I don't fight against it, either.

Our eyes stay locked on each other. The tension between us is so thick that I can feel it weighing down my chest. It's that same familiar feeling that comes with figuring out if you should kiss someone. Even though we've already kissed—several times, in fact—it feels different this time.

It feels like foreplay.

It's empowering to receive what feels like confirmation that the feelings are mutual. My nerves melt, overpowered by my desire to take the bait.

"Is it too forward of me to say I wish we weren't stuck at an airport tonight?" I ask, my voice low.

Emmy only shakes her head in response, no words necessary. Her eyes travel down to my lips and I'm suddenly right back in that bathroom. I can feel her hands on me, my body against mine. I can still hear her words: *I wish you could feel how wet I am.*

I want to kiss her but I don't trust myself to keep things appropriate for a public space. I know how quickly it will heat up; one kiss could never possibly be enough. This is especially true when it's so easy for me to convince myself that we're mostly hidden. It's not true—in the same way we can see everyone, everyone can see us. But it's so quiet in our specific gate that it's like our own little oasis.

"How far do you live from here?" Emmy asks.

I shake my head. "Too far."

She nods. "Me too."

We're at a standstill. Nowhere for us to go, nothing for us to do except want each other.

I can't remember the last time I was in a situation like this, where I have access to the person and it's mutual but we can't do anything about it. Normally, it's some kind of date night— a bar, a restaurant. We're in a situation where we have a place to go when we both give each other the look and know it's time to leave. Even if it's just a car, there's always *somewhere* to go.

The anticipation, the waiting, the needing but not being able to get to her, is killing me. I'm certain it's the hungriest I've ever been before. It's the kind of need that comes without the promise of release, the kind of need that so quickly becomes all consuming.

Emmy readjusts her arm and reaches for my hand. Our open palms find each other.

"Is this when I'm supposed to talk all about how your hands are *so* big?" Emmy teases.

"Oh, absolutely," I say, as if her hands aren't only a couple of centimeters smaller than mine. We're nearly the same height —I only have an inch or two on her. And our builds are virtually the same. The only difference is I've started flattening out my breasts with a binder when I can.

"They're soft," she says.

"My hands?" I ask, a little surprised. "That's all that working on a computer. Hands that have never done hard labor once in their life."

Emmy throws her head back with laughter. It's the sweetest sound I've ever heard. We've been giggling together seemingly since the second we initially crossed paths, but this is something different. It's deeply genuine, the kind of laugh that surprises both of us.

I find myself smiling at her in amusement. I'm genuinely prideful over being able to get her to laugh like that. I've never considered myself to be someone who is particularly funny and it's never necessarily my goal to make people laugh, but I won't complain when it happens. Especially when it's Emmy.

"The opposite of farm hands," she says.

"Small town hands in the sense that they're mostly used for driving twenty minutes to a grocery store, not small town hands in the sense of physical work,"

"I think I have social media hands," Emmy admits. "Former Tumblr user and poetry writing hands."

I snort out a laugh. "Also very soft."

"Thank you," she says. We naturally weave our hands together again, dropping them into my lap. "I'm glad we can check off *compared hand sizes* from our list of stereotypical lesbian date activities."

"Oh, this is a date?" I ask.

Emmy nearly rolls her eyes at me with a smile at her lips, leaning her head onto my shoulder. "I'm not even going to dignify that with a response."

I pull her closer to me, our bodies melting together like we've known each other for much longer than a few hours. Something about all of this is so deeply romantic—the fire pits, the cold weather as an excuse to curl up close to each other, the hustle and bustle around us but the quiet of the moment between us.

My chest feels warm, simultaneously light and full with how well this is all going. There's something about being around Emmy that makes me feel excited but also safe. It's surreal and somewhat new to me, and I know that it most likely has to do with the fact that it's all so new. There's no history to get caught up in, no familiarity to fall back on, so it can all feel exciting. But the safe part, the way that it feels like I can say just about anything to her and the way we work together, is something else entirely. It's making me realize that I'm not sure I've ever felt this exact feeling with someone else before.

I can feel Emmy's body gently move with each of her breaths. All of the chemicals in my brain are going haywire. It's been an admittedly long time since I've just held someone, and especially held someone not in the context of immediately following sex.

In some ways, this is following sex—or whatever foreplay it was that Emmy and I had gotten up to in the bathroom. But this feels different. It feels like casual intimacy, not the intimacy that comes with being in bed together.

Emmy turns to look at me I'm overwhelmed by my desire to kiss her. The thought comes so naturally now. Rather than wondering if she'll kiss me back, my brain just immediately jumps to wanting to go all in. I feel more certain now that she'll reciprocate.

My eyes fall down onto her lips and the electric charge between us turns up to one hundred. Her eyes travel over my face, dancing between my eyes and my lips.

I know the cues well enough; I can read our body language. But something about sitting in the moment for a second feels good. I like the anticipation and watching Emmy's lips part, the two of us moving the tiniest bit toward each other. I can *really* tell now that we're both on the same exact page. I like knowing that she's thinking about me, that she looks hungry for me.

Not wanting the moment to pass, I lean toward her until we're only a breath apart. When our lips finally brush, it feels like setting off a million fireworks. Neediness blooms between my legs in a way, even stronger this time around. The more we tease each other, the harder it becomes to control myself and the thoughts I'm having.

The kiss can't be much more than a quick peck because we're in public, but something about that makes it even hotter. There's a tortuous, delicious pleasure in knowing I can only have part of Emmy and that what I really want to do with her is off limits.

We pull our faces apart but our bodies stay as close together as we can comfortably have them. My mind is racing with possibilities—we go back to the bathroom, we hide somewhere else in the airport, we sneak around outside. It even crosses my mind that it might be worth it to just say fuck it and see if there's a hotel room we can go to, but that doesn't seem likely.

"Can I say something embarrassing?" Emmy asks, her voice quiet.

My heart races, wondering what she might say. "You can say anything," I tell her.

"All of the jokes about the Denver Airport kind of scare me a little bit, but knowing that I'll be spending the night with you makes it less scary," she says.

The comment is so surprising, so left field, that I burst out laughing. I can tell from Emmy's sheepish face that a tiny part of her really genuinely means it, but she's also teasing. "You're scared of the Denver Airport?"

"I mean, like, not really but also...yes," she says. "Don't you agree there's something strange about this place? I think there is. And it's weird that it seems like it's the only airport in America that has so many weird conspiracy theories around it. It makes me think that something about this place must be kind of weird at least, right?"

"Is it really the only one?"

"It's probably not, but it's the one I always think of. And there's that horse in the front too with the eyes. The vibe here is weird," Emmy says, keeping her voice low as if she thinks someone—or something—might overhear.

I laugh again, keeping her close and our hands interwoven. "It's technically a mustang but in case it happens to come to life overnight, I'll protect you."

"I don't know if you'd be able to but I'm glad you'd have my back in case some sort of supernatural incident happens while we're here."

"We just won't wander too far and accidentally end up down a weird side hallway or something."

"Oh, absolutely not. I have no interest in being any places other than the clearly designated ones."

I look over at her, strands of hair framing her face, her lips partially turned up in a seemingly always-present smile. I brush a piece of her hair out of her face out of instinct, wanting to see more of her. Her skin is so soft; I let my thumb linger for just a second, wanting to take advantage of any second of contact I can get.

She flicks her brown eyes up toward me and I'm almost overwhelmed by how attractive she is. I'm nervous all over again for just a beat, and then a flood of warmth comes in reminding me that she is ridiculously beautiful, but she's also choosing to be here with me. The nerves should only be excitement.

"Is it too soon to say something along the lines of *it's been a long time since I've enjoyed hanging out with someone new this much*?" Emmy asks.

I shake my head. "No, because I feel the same way," I say. "I like talking to you."

"You like talking to me?" Emmy teases. "Kind of embarrassing to admit."

"I'll be embarrassed."

Her lips twist up in an amused smirk and she has to avert her eyes away from me for a beat. I like that she wears her expressions so plainly; it feels like I know everything she's thinking as she's thinking it. She doesn't feel the need to bury everything down. If I get her flustered, I know it so plainly. It's hot.

I'm suddenly filled with such an intense urge to be with her that I feel overwhelmed by it. I want nothing more than to kiss her deeply, to get her out of her clothes. I want her breathless and naked and wet between her legs, all for me to enjoy. The hunger is deep and I know I won't feel completely satiated ever again until I have her. Even if we only get one night together, it's worth it to me.

"Can I take you to the hotel nearby?" I ask and as soon as the words come out of my mouth, I'm embarrassed by them. I worry I asked them the wrong way or that my intentions aren't clear enough or that I'm completely misreading the situation. I want to take them back almost immediately but I also…don't. I know I'll regret it if I don't ask. And watching as the winter sun completely sets and the airport gets enveloped in darkness, time is running out. My window of opportunity will only be so long, especially if we have to be back here to wait on standby for early flights out.

"Do you think we'll be able to get a room?" Emmy asks.

My chest lights up with hope and the thrill of her not shutting down the idea. It might not be exactly a yes, but it's something. "I want to at least try."

Emmy's eyes dance around my face again and her lips part slightly. She looks so sweet sitting there in my sweatshirt, but my gut is telling me we're the same filthy thoughts abour what we'd do if we were alone right now.

"Fuck it," Emmy says. "Let's go."

chapter seven

EMMY and I gather our things. I stand up from the floor, offering my hand to help her up.

"Do you want your sweatshirt back for the journey?" she asks.

I shake my head. "It looks better on you than it does on me."

I love the look on her face as the words set in. I can't get enough of making her smile, catching her off guard occasionally. She might've been the one bold enough to invite me into the bathroom with her, but she's not the only bold one here.

I take her overhead back into my hand before she can grab it, rolling hers on one side and mine on the other.

"You don't have to take my bag," she says.

"But I want to," I say, because it really is that simple. My immediate instinct is always to step in where I can. I know there's an extra impulse with Emmy because I generally like her so much and also find her attractive, but it's my baseline. I feel an urge to make people's lives easier in whatever way I can, including carrying shit. I'm prone to taking out my friends' trash and emptying their dishwashers, too, when we're waiting for the pregame to start.

Emmy and I walk side-by-side, passing gate after gate. There are so many people around doing the best they can to get comfortable. I have a feeling Emmy and I will end up joining them because chances are low that there are rooms still available at the hotel. But I'd rather try than assume we're completely out of luck. And the hotel is in the airport, anyway, so it's just an added step to the adventure.

As we're walking, the reality of the situation seems to suddenly sink in all at once. I feel *extremely* aware of what's going to come next if we're lucky enough to get a room. It's the same feeling of anticipation that comes with agreeing to go home together after a first date. It's exciting and nerve wracking all at once. I can't wait to take her clothes off and am practically buzzing at the thought, but I also think of all of the other parts of it. We could have zero chemistry in bed. Or she could think I'm bad. I've never gotten a negative review, but it doesn't mean it won't come eventually.

But after the moment we shared in the bathroom, I doubt any time we spend alone together in a hotel room could be boring. I have a feeling with all of the anticipation we've built up, it'll end up being some of the best sex I've ever had.

We're quietly walking to the hotel in a way that feels comfortable but a little contemplative. I can feel in the way we stand next to each other that we're both thinking about the same exact thing. When Emmy's eyes flick over and meet mine, we share a small smile. Her eyes hang just the tiniest bit, giving a look that's nothing short of lustful. I can't tell if it's intentional or not, if I'm just so wildly attracted to her that she could look at me however she wanted to and I would fall to my knees.

After an elevator ride and a little more walking, we arrive at the entrance. It's a zoo, people hovering around on their phones, rushing around to find each other, doing the best they can to not pick a fight with a loved one. Everyone is talking hurriedly about how the rooms are booked out and they need a hotel anywhere else in the general area. It sounds like the roads are bad, so there's hesitation to leave.

My heart sinks at the scene. I had in some ways prepared myself for it, but I had also been trying to hold onto some hope that maybe the universe is looking out for us. Part of me feels like we deserve this, even if it's entitled to believe that to be the case. We don't deserve a hotel room just because we're two horny twenty-somethings who might never cross paths again.

Emmy beelines toward reception and I have to bite back at a smile at the thought of why she's rushing over there so quickly. I find the confidence of it all sexy, too; she's not overwhelmed by the chaos or the people around. She really means business.

"Hi, do you have—"

"No rooms," the receptionist says quickly, barely even looking at her. It's obvious she's exhausted; I can only imagine the day she's had. The only people who've had it worse than the people stuck waiting for their flights are the people who've had to *deal* with the people stuck waiting for their flights.

"Nothing? No cancellations? No no-shows? There are probably at least a couple of people who couldn't make it for their reservation because of the snow," Emmy says optimistically.

"Rooms are booked out."

"It's our anniversary," Emmy pleads. She's admittedly not doing a great job of selling it—good to know that she's a terrible liar—but I step closer to her and put my hand around my waist to try and make it seem more convincing.

If the receptionist was uninterested before, she's somehow even more uninterested now. I'm sure she's heard pleas of all kinds—anniversaries, birthdays, people who need to get home urgently for one reason or another and would just like a comfortable bed to sleep in in the meantime.

Emmy steps back and turns to me. "The bar?" she offers.

THE BAR IS ALMOST as chaotic as the front lobby but it's moderately more manageable, probably because people can't have their kids running around inside of it. There are a couple of large groups huddled together. One group is wearing matching themed shirts announcing *Carol's 65!* I'm guessing based on their tropical themed attire that they're trying to *leave* Colorado to celebrate somewhere much warmer.

Across the way, I see another large group that is not wearing coordinated attire and doesn't strike me as a group of people who know each other at all. I overhear in bits and pieces that they're talking about how to get home from here— weighing the pros and cons of driving, checking other airports in the area to see if they can get out of town that way.

"It's a mess," Emmy says.

I take her hand and lead her toward the bar, where there are fortunately two seats that have just opened. They're practically still warm when we sit down.

We tuck our rollerbags between our knees and under the counter, our limbs brushing against each other. It's just as thrilling as before but in a slightly different way. Even though it's all still new, we've spent hours collectively together at this point. The excitement isn't in what's going to happen next; it's the anticipation of waiting, knowing the wait will have been worth it.

"Can I get you a drink?" I offer.

"Are you going to spill it on me again?" Emmy teases.

"I don't have enough sweatshirts to offer you to keep that trend going," I say and she laughs. "I'll keep my hands firmly planted on my knees to avoid any potential mishaps."

"Of course," Emmy says, her lips turning up in a smile. The look she gives me makes my heart go nuts in my chest and my palms sweaty. It's so casual, just a quick glance over with her round brown eyes, but it's permanently etched into my memory.

In an instant, I imagine us in a hotel room together, her looking down at me through partially lowered lids. Her hips bucking against my lips, her weight on me. I imagine all of the different things we could do with a full uninterrupted night together. There's absolutely no reason for me to have brought an emergency strap to a wedding, but I'm suddenly regretting the oversight.

My chest sinks a little bit at the realization that we won't get that tonight. And we might not ever get that. As I watch Emmy flag down the bartender, I think about how I should just ask her if she plans on seeing me again, if she'd potentially want to. It's an easy enough question and it shouldn't be that big of a deal to ask—it's not like I'll ever see her again outside of this if I embarrass myself.

But I can tell I actually *like* Emmy and like spending time around her because the idea of rejection is actually scary. It's not to say that I'm immune to rejection, but I'm not necessarily afraid to hit on someone at a bar or offer to buy someone a drink. It feels easy, casual—no strings attached.

And then here comes Emmy—effortlessly beautiful and electric. There's a specific kind of spark in her that's making all of my usual moves feel stupid. I've never felt so self-aware before, but it's in the best way. It has nothing to do with the way she's treating me and everything to do with how aware I am that she is exactly what I've been looking for. I don't want to risk screwing this up.

I flag down the bartender and order us the same drinks as before. The entire time, I can feel Emmy gazing at me out of the corner of my eye. It makes me blush so hot I can feel it radiating off my skin and I'm grateful it's pretty dark in here.

It's hard not to think about what it was like in the bathroom with her. The teasing, the touching. The way her lips felt against mine.

Part of me can't help but wonder if it's just the thrill of it that makes this so intriguing. I can have her, but not really. She's so close but so far from me. We're one already-booked hotel room, one trip, away from being able to actually be together.

But I can feel it's different. This isn't like when I'm told by my friends that someone is off limits; it's something else entirely. Something new.

I consider just asking for her number now, or maybe asking her if she thinks we'll see each other again. The least logical part of me is dying to know.

I turn to look at Emmy and when she locks eyes with me, I feel so incredibly uncool for a moment that I almost feel embarrassed. My palms are the tiniest bit sweaty and my heart is racing. I'm starting to reach a point where I'm pretty sure I *need* that drink to keep me level.

But I also know the drink is what's going to put me at risk of saying something so incredibly stupid that I won't be able to fix it. Something like *hey, do you have a super intense crush on me too or is this feeling not mutual?*

Our knees brush against each other and stay this time. We keep the contact going, neither of us moving. I can feel the electric charge going between us. I'm aware of every muscle in my body. I wish I wasn't so self-aware; it'd be so much easier to navigate this if I could just stay calm. But I'm having a harder and harder time the more time passes and the closer we are to inevitably going our separate ways.

All of the confidence from earlier—the version of me that was capable of asking her if she wanted to get a hotel room with me—is completely gone. All that's left is the realization that we're not getting a hotel room tonight and the only next possible option is hoping she'll want to see me again when our trips are done.

I take a deep breath, bracing myself for the inevitable. Maybe it's not actually now or never, but it kind of feels that way. We're not getting a hotel so we have to figure out what will come next and the only way to know is by asking.

I look over at Emmy, who's looking ahead curiously at something on the TV. The way the light of the bar illuminates her makes me nervous all over again. Her hair falls just the right way. Even her posture is cool. She's so calm and relaxed, just taking a sip of her drink and somehow looking like the coolest person there.

My mouth goes dry and I know I can't ask. There's no way I'll be able to push myself to start that conversation of what we're supposed to do now. Not with her looking like that. I'd rather get the rest of the night with her and not fuck it up than spend the rest of the evening wondering why I couldn't just be patient.

"What are you thinking about?" Emmy asks, turning to look at me. "I can feel your eyes on me."

I blush hard and hot, mortified by how obvious I was being. "Oh. Just..."

Emmy throws a teasing smile in my direction. "I don't actually need to know. I just wanted to see if I could get you to blush."

I laugh, relieved and embarrassed all at once. "You don't have to try and make me blush."

She turns to look at me, propping her head up with her hands. Her brown eyes shine with warmth. She looks so beautiful that I'm half-tempted to propose to her right there, never wanting to lose sight of her.

"Oh, hello!"

It takes me a second to break out of my daze. I'm so caught up in Emmy that I don't realize that Rosa and Charlie are standing nearby. They look just as surprised to see us as I'm sure we look.

"Hey!" Emmy greets them warmly, as if we've all known each other for years. "What are you doing here?"

"This is the hotel we booked the room for. Good thing we though to jump on it early, aye?" Charlie says lightly, gesturing to everyone around us.

"Oh, wow! What a fun surprise," Emmy says. "We weren't so lucky. Neither of us could figure out what we wanted to do so now we're stuck in limbo. We'll probably just camp out on one of the floors."

Rosa's brows furrow slightly. "You girls can't do that."

"Oh, it's no problem. Everything is booked up and there's nowhere for us to go. It's just part of the adventure."

Charlie and Rosa look at each other. Charlie then digs into his pocket and pulls out two room keys. "We've only checked in, we haven't even been up to the room yet. We were planning on wandering as much as we can before everything shuts down and we're stuck in the room for the rest of the evening. And then when we saw the weather report, we decided we might as well just try and celebrate elsewhere. There's just enough of a slowdown right now for us to get home. Our son is already on the way to pick us up."

"Oh, we can't—" I say, realizing where he's going with this.

Rosa smiles, holding her husband's arm. "We insist. We don't need to go anywhere. We'll just take the loss of the trip. But you two have real plans and destinations to get to. You should stay at the hotel and at least be able to rest before you head off on your trips."

"This is really kind, but we can't possibly. You're sure you feel comfortable leaving the airport tonight? I've heard conditions still aren't great," Emmy says.

"We're taking advantage of the window we have now. It's a couple of hours of quiet," Charlie says. "We've been in Colorado for long enough to know how to navigate this kind of weather."

"Please, we insist. We'd want someone to do the same thing for our kids if they were stuck here. If we can give you peace and quiet for even a couple of hours, we're happy to," Rosa says.

Emmy and I look at each other, neither of us having any additional words of protest to offer. I'm still not sure I actually want to take them up on this. A hotel room here isn't cheap on a normal day. I can only imagine what rates probably look like with snow and increased need. It's way too much for me to try and help cover, and I don't feel right accepting it as a gift.

"You're really sure?" Emmy asks.

"Yes, absolutely. We came here to get a drink to wait out our ride, but it feels like fate we ran into the two of you," she says. "Go take a hot shower and get off your feet for a little. It's too late for us to get a refund on anything anyway, so it'll just be an expense we paid for and wasted."

"You really don't want it?" I ask, echoing Emmy.

"We just want to go home with everything going on. We're retirees, we can vacation whenever. We don't need to deal with all of this mess," Charlie says. He hands the keys off to Emmy. "Enjoy your trips."

They both offer us warm smiles and then head off, like two very generous mystical beings disappearing into the fog.

"Um," Emmy says, looking at the plastic keycards in her hand.

"I guess we're getting the room," I say.

"They really don't want us to pay them back or anything?"

Emmy asks. "Really? Do you think this is some kind of weird scam? Or set-up?"

I laugh. "I don't think so, I think they just might be...nice people?"

Emmy lips turn up in a smile and then shakes her head. "I mean, what are the odds? This is so crazy."

"Feeling the holiday spirit I guess?"

"In mid-February?"

Emmy shrugs and we both laugh.

"I mean, should we go see the room? Since we have it?" I ask.

chapter eight

EMMY and I finish off our drinks quickly and I flag down the bartender while Emmy gathers our things. As soon as we pay, we head back into the hotel lobby and beeline to the elevators.

It's still packed and busy, but it feels a little less overwhelming now that I know we're escaping from it all. I'm surprised by how quickly the switch flipped in my brain since I'm usually not someone who can easily accept gifts, but I also know not to dwell on it too long. Wasting the room in the name of pride is pointless; we might as well use it since we can.

"What's the room number?" I ask.

Emmy flips over the little hotel-provided card holder containing the keys. "423."

"Perfect," I say. Emmy swipes the card reader and I press the number to go to the fourth floor.

When the elevator doors close, reality really hits me. This isn't just getting an escape from the noise; it's a way for us to be somewhere alone together.

Emmy and I look at each other. We're alone in the elevator —completely alone for the first time since the bathroom. We seem to have the same exact thought at the same time. Warmth blooms between my legs and my cheeks flush as if she's somehow going to know exactly what I'm thinking.

But based on the look on her face—the way her full lips are parted slightly and she's looking up at me with heavy eyelids—it seems like we're on the same page. It's not embarrassing for me to be thinking about her fully naked in the hotel bed. It's so easy to imagine what her moans would sound like and the way her hands would feel in my hair.

The elevator dings as the doors open and we both jump and break eye contact as if pulled out of daze.

Neither of us say anything. The closer we get to the room, the more my mouth feels uncomfortably, embarrassingly dry. I'm thinking of every worst case scenario—I get too embarrassed to actually make a move, I try and make a move and I suck in bed, I accidentally do something to offend her or something weird.

I realize as we're walking silently down the hallway, our bags and shoes shuffling against the hotel carpet, that I have no concerns about how Emmy will be. Not one cell in my body is worried about her doing something weird or her being bad in bed. And with complete honesty, I'm right to feel that way. I know how she was when we were in the bathroom together. She's hot and she knows it; I only need to worry about myself.

And I am *definitely* worrying about myself.

I swipe the key in the door and push it open, holding it so Emmy can get by first.

"Thank you," she says. I can only nod, hovering for a second as I watch her entire the room.

I can't even believe this is really happening.

I'm half convinced this is some kind of elaborate dream. I must've fallen asleep somewhere on the floor of the airport. There's no way we're actually here.

But I can feel the weight of my bag on my shoulders and in my hand. I can smell Emmy's perfume, clear as day.

All of it is real.

I step into the hotel room and softly close the door behind me.

Emmy puts her bags down on the desk and looks at the single bed that's in the room. It occurs to me up until now that we'd gotten a room from a married couple; of course, there would only be one bed.

"Oh, I—" I say, looking at the bed.

"I don't mind if you don't," Emmy says easily. She turns back to look at me with a small smile at her lips.

Everything in me melts. I feel drawn to her. I'm desperate to be as close to her as possible, to kiss her again.

I step toward her, putting my bags down on the ground. Emmy's lips are turned up in a small smile, her lips parted again.

"Can I—"

"Yes," Emmy says.

I don't waste a moment. I lean in and kiss her again and it's even better than I remembered it being. I hold her close to me, kissing her deeply. It's the freest we've been able to be since we met. For the first time, there's no one around. There are no expectations around time, there's no urgency.

I trace my thumb over Emmy's jaw and bring one of my hands to her waist. I pull her against me so our bodies are touching as she puts her arms around my neck.

Kissing her feels like the most natural thing in the world. It only takes me about a second to adjust and then I know exactly how to match her rhythm. Just from kissing alone, I can feel that I'm soaking wet. I'm hungry but not desperate; if this is all that I get from her, I'll happily take it. I'll be able to live the rest of my life knowing that we shared this moment together.

Her mouth opens as her hands trace over my arms and back. When she slides her hands beneath the material of my shirt, I nearly gasp at the sensation. There's no use in trying to play it cool or hide my desire at this point; we're already here.

There's something freeing about that. My nerves melt away in an instant. I'm here with a hot girl who wants me at least as badly as I want her. I won't gain anything by being nonchalant or acting like I'm not excited about it. Every part of me is singing out to her touch. I want to lean into that. I want to let her know.

I gently guide her toward the bed, wanting to gauge exactly how far she wants to take this. In response, she grips onto my shirt and pulls me down onto the bed with her.

I position myself between her legs, continuing to kiss her with everything I have. I feel like a teenager who's exploring kissing a girl for the first time. I want to makeout with her for hours, excited by the prospect of maybe getting to feel her up if I get lucky.

Emmy lets out a small moan as I slide one of my hands up her shirt. She kisses from my lips to my cheek and then down to my neck, taking her time. She glides her tongue against my skin. I'm glad we're already on the bed because the sensation is enough to make me weak in the knees.

"Fuck, Emmy," I breathe out and Emmy whimpers needily in response.

Her hands wander up my shirt, trailing my back. She gently scratches her nails and I'm now *really* wishing I'd had the foresight to bring the strap.

"I want to continue this," Emmy says breathlessly, "but I need to shower first before we go any further."

I kiss her neck, moving up toward her ear. She giggles, which then turns into a moan and she grips onto me even tighter.

"You don't *need* to shower," I say.

"I want to. I feel...sweaty. And gross. There's something evil about airport air," she says. "I promise I'll be quick. I just want to be able to actually enjoy this without spending the whole time thinking about how I feel like I smell bad."

"You don't smell bad," I say. I pull away from her and we lock eyes. "I think you smell really good, actually. But I won't stop you if you want to. I get it."

Her gaze drops, taking me in. Her eyes dance between my eyes and my lips.

She groans. "I don't want to stop."

"We don't have to," I say.

"I know," she says.

"No, I mean, we don't have to," I say and nod my head toward the direction of the bathroom.

Emmy's eyes light up. "You'd want to?"

"See you naked? Yes, absolutely."

She laughs. "There's definitely enough space for two in there."

"I'm down," I say. "You know, if I smell bad, you can just say it. You don't have to jump through hoops to communicate it."

Emmy catches my teasing tone. She laughs again and rolls her eyes. "I promise that you don't smell bad. But this would be a clever way of getting you into a shower if you did. I appreciate that you think I'm that smart."

"I might not know you that well but I think you are that smart," I say and then kiss her again. She wraps her arms around me and we get lost in kissing again, physically unable to stay away from each other.

It's unclear how much time has passed when we finally break apart again. Emmy then takes my hand and leads me toward the bathroom.

The bathroom isn't anything glamorous, just like the rest of the hotel. It's generic but nice enough—definitely better than toughing it out on the floor of the airport.

Emmy leans into the shower to turn on the water and

pulls me toward her again. We kiss with the kind of desperation typically reserved for people who haven't been able to kiss for a long time.

I understand the rhythm now and it feels natural to me to kiss her. My brain is completely empty in the best way. Everything is about her, her, her.

I pull her sweatshirt and shirt over her head as she reaches for the button to my pants. Her skin is impossibly warm and soft. I weave my hands through her hair as she tilts her head back, allowing me more access to her neck. She grips onto me, letting out moans that become increasingly less shy.

It's not until the bathroom mirror is fogged with steam that I remember that we're supposed to be taking a shower. We strip off the rest of our clothes, Emmy standing in a cute pair of panties and me in boxers.

Emmy is perfect. Every inch of her. She practically glows in the bathroom lighting, her skin so smooth it doesn't even seem possible. Her breasts are round and perky, her nipples raised, hardened mounds.

I trail down toward her stomach, which is smooth and practically begging me to touch. I want to wrap my arms around her waist, want to hold her close to me. I can already imagine what it would feel like for us to fall asleep together, our bodies wrapped up in each other.

I step forward and flatten my hands against her back. I trail them forward, exploring as much of her body as I can. We're not even kissing at this point; we're just holding onto each other closely, listening to the sounds of the other person breathing as the water runs.

I reach for the waist of her underwear and slowly pull them down, trailing them down her legs. I take my time. With every passing second, I want her even more. The longer we put this off, the more I feel like I might actually explode from desire. I've never needed anyone like this before.

When Emmy's underwear drops to the floor, she kicks them off. She's completely naked in front of me now.

"Wow." I exhale. The reaction is so genuine that it comes out before I can think about it or get embarrassed. But I'm not going to be shy about a ridiculously hot woman standing naked in front of me.

Emmy's lips turn up in a smile. She kisses me and then steps into the shower, turning to look back over her shoulder at me.

I follow quickly behind her, dropping my briefs in a second. I step into the shower and the second I feel the water on me, I realize how good of a decision this was.

"Oh, that feels incredible," I moan. Emmy laughs and steps aside so I stand fully under the head of the shower. "You're a genius. I needed this."

"I think we both needed this," Emmy says, watching me with an amused smile.

I reach for the complimentary body wash and offer some to Emmy before pouring it out in my hands. We take our time, luxuriating in the hot water and the nice body wash.

"I didn't realize how cold I was until now," Emmy says.

"I can't believe we were going to sleep on the airport floor."

"I would've slept anywhere with you."

Her tone is mostly teasing, but the comment is so unexpectedly sweet that it takes me by surprise. It actually manages to render me speechless. "Oh yeah?" I say, the only thing I can manage.

"You really think I'm going to give up a night with the hottest person I've ever seen? All so I can suffer, cold and alone, somewhere in an airport? I'd much rather hangout with you."

"Oh, great—so I'm better than being alone overnight in an airport? Hard standard."

Emmy laughs easily. "You know what I mean."

I smile at her as she rinses off, her head tilted back under the water. She's effortlessly beautiful in a way that makes it impossible to look away from her. Everything feels so right, it's like we've been doing this forever.

"It's weird how comfortable I feel around you," I say. "Or maybe not actually weird. But it's unusual for me."

Emmy steps out from under the water. She looks straight out of a Sports Illustrated shoot; it nearly takes my breath away. "It's unusual for me too. I'm never really that...forward. I don't know what came over me in the airport."

A rush of warmth floods my chest. I haven't been holding onto hope that I'm special in some way to her, but it's nice to hear that I actually have been this whole time.

"Yeah?"

"Yeah," she says. "I saw an opportunity. It's one of those like...be bold on vacation type of things. You'll probably never have the chance again. I see why people like to do random flings while they're traveling for work and things like that."

I try to hide the disappointment on my face. Maybe I am special but that doesn't mean that I'm who she wants. Maybe this is just the start of her leaning into a new thing of casual hook ups. Maybe she's not even looking for something meaningful.

And why would I ever think that she was? We're two people who met and flirted and fooled around. There's no reason to assume this is supposed to be anything more.

Emmy and I switch off so I can rinse. I try not to act weird but I can tell that I probably am. Right now is absolutely not the time to be having any kind of feelings other than excitement about the naked woman with me. But there they are— taking up space and making it impossible for me to just be *chill*.

"All good?" Emmy asks, throwing a flirty look over her shoulder.

I feel—irrationally—sick to my stomach thinking about her flirting with someone else. I imagine all of the hot women she met before me, picturing them as cooler and more interesting and stronger. They probably did all sorts of things Emmy bragged to her friends about and went to graduate school. And they all had better hair that doesn't stick up in all directions when they sleep on it, like mine does.

"Yeah, all good," I say.

Emmy turns off the water and I reach out to grab a towel for her and then for me. We start drying off, Emmy still tossing looks in my direction. I want to be able to match the energy and offer the same thing back that I'd already been offering, but it's hard for me to get back to where I was. I'm completely in my head now. I'm miles ahead, comparing myself to other masc-presenting women Emmy slept with who I'm completely making up.

After mostly drying off, Emmy exits the bathroom. A blast of cold air rushes into the bathroom and the steam from the shower escapes.

I quickly towel off my hair and wrap myself in the towel, patting myself dry.

"It's cold out here!" Emmy calls out from somewhere in the hotel room. I can't see her anymore; all I can see is me in the bathroom, standing with the towel wrapped around me. I feel a little ridiculous. I can't remember the last time someone would've showered with me and seen me in a towel like this. It sits oddly against my frame, the closest I've gotten to wearing a dress since childhood.

I step out of the bathroom, maneuvering past Emmy who is digging through her bag. She has only a fresh pair of underwear on, the rest of her naked. Even from a distance, I can see that she has goosebumps.

I turn away so I don't get distracted and instead focus on getting clothes out of my own suitcase.

For the first time since we crossed paths, the air between me and Emmy feels weird. I'm certain that it's just me who's feeling it and it's all because *I'm* feeling weird, but I hate it all the same. I just wish my brain would shut off for a moment and let me enjoy getting to know Emmy. First, I'm obsessed with what will happen next and how much this means to her. Then, when I start to make peace with going with the flow, I have to fixate on exes.

I've never really struggled with jealousy before, but there's no hiding from the reality now. It's very obvious what's going on and I hate it.

I get dressed with my back turned to Emmy. I can hear her opening and closing various little bottles of skincare.

When I get my clothes on and turn around, Emmy is turned to look at me. She has a matching loungewear set on, her damp hair moved away from her face and tucked behind her ears.

"What's up?" she asks. It's non-accusatory. Her tone is surprisingly gentle and curious, almost playful. A question like that would typically make my stomach drop; it's the kind of thing someone says when they can tell something is weird. I tend to hear it when I'm involved with a girl who I'm not really interested in seeing but don't have it in me to get out of it. Communication hasn't exactly been my strong suit in that way. It's hard to have to deliver bad news.

And even though Emmy's words don't trigger the same reaction in me as hearing it in the past, I still really don't like communication.

"What do you mean?" I ask.

"This is the quietest you've been since we met. We've barely spoken since we got out of the shower," she says. She looks at me, meeting my eyes. "It's okay if you don't want to do this. I'm happy to sleep somewhere else, too."

"No, no, that's not it," I say. I run my hands through my damp hair and sit down on the edge of the hotel bed. "I just…" I trail off, not knowing what to say. I'm mortified that it's so obvious. I have no idea how to explain to her, someone who might as well be a stranger, that I think I have a crush on her and I'm jealous because of it. It feels ridiculous.

Emmy walks over toward me, leaning against the edge of the desk across from me. "I'm being serious, Harper. Nothing has to happen. You're allowed to change your mind whenever."

"It's not that," I say. "I really want to have sex with you. As long as you want to, at least," I quickly add. "I don't want to be presumptuous."

"Is this when you tell me you've had a girlfriend at home this whole time?" she asks. She's still lightly teasing but there's a little bit of a tinge to it. It sounds like maybe she is kind of worried that's a possibility.

"Oh, absolutely not," I say, laughing. Emmy laughs and lets out what almost sounds like a sigh of relief. "No. I've been…very single for a hot second. Embarrassingly single." I take a deep breath. "Which I think might be part of the issue."

"Tell me more."

"Oh," I say, not expecting her genuine tone or interest. I don't know what else I could've expected from her, though. "Um. It's embarrassing."

"It doesn't have to be. It's okay."

I take a deep breath and tilt my head toward the ceiling. I think over everything that's transpired since we met. I'm not even sure how much time has passed. Nothing feels real with Emmy. We could've known each other for three years or three hours and I wouldn't have known the difference. The sun being down and the sky being completely dark now is the only indicator I have that time has moved.

"I've really liked getting to know you," I say, forcing the words out of my mouth. I keep my head still tilted away from her, not wanting to see her reaction. "This—to me, at least—has felt like a great first date and if we'd met on, like, a dating app or something, I would invite you home and ask you on a second date."

Emmy is quiet for so long that I genuinely start to get nervous. I look at her, expecting a response similar to one I've given girls in the past. *I just don't see this as anything serious. I don't feel the same way.*

Instead, Emmy looks at me with an expression I can't read. It seems almost like she's trying to keep a smile down, but that feels like wishful thinking on my part.

"That's it?" she asks and then breaks out into the smile I'd come to love seeing so much. "Do you have a crush on me?"

"I...maybe. Yes. Next level up from an airport crush, whatever that would be," I say, still unable to maintain eye contact with her. I have too many feelings swirling inside of me to know how to actually feel. I'm nervous, shy, excited, hopeful. The one thing I know for sure is that I want her so badly.

Emmy squeals and practically leaps onto me, wrapping her arms around my neck. She kisses me, taking me by surprise. I hold onto her and make sure she doesn't slip off of my lap and onto the floor.

"I have a crush on you, too," Emmy says. "I would let you take me out for a second date."

"Yeah?" I ask, my lips turning up in a smile.

She kisses me again, pushing me down onto the bed. Her hair falls over one of her shoulders. "Yes. Absolutely."

We melt into each other, getting lost in kissing all over again. I place my hands on her lower back and waist. Thinking about what's hiding under her clothes gets me immediately wet all over again. I know with absolute certainty I want her more than I've ever wanted anyone before. There's just something about her.

It's not to say it'll be forever, but I want to see where things will go from here.

"Is that it?" Emmy asks in a light and sing-song-y voice. "Anything else? Or just harboring secret feelings from me? Because you were being awfully weird…"

I laugh. "It's, you know, like…" I groan. "I don't know. I like you. And it's making me get all in my head about, like, people you've dated before and where I fit into all of it and if you'd even be interested in me in return. And you mentioned how fun this all was, meeting a stranger and fooling around with them."

"It can be fun and I can decide I don't necessarily want to do it again," Emmy says. Just like before, her tone is understanding and calm rather than defensive. "The two can coexist. And also, don't worry about exes. They're not with me anymore for a reason." She pauses and looks at me. "Plus, you're *hot*. And you're nice. You want me to believe that you don't have any women in your phone, waiting for you to come home?"

I laugh. "I promise there is not one person excited to see me when I get home. Maybe my roommate's cat. But it's been one thing after another. I've had a running streak of pretty terrible dating luck. This has been a nice change of pace."

Emmy's eyes dance over my face. Her lips suddenly turn up in a smile and she stands up, sitting in my lap and straddling my legs. She wraps her arms around my neck and I put my hands on her waist to keep her up—and close to me.

"Oh yeah? I'm a nice change of pace?"

"Very nice," I say. "The best kind."

Emmy brings her hands to my damp hair and gently yanks, tilting my head up toward her. If it wasn't already wet,

I'd definitely be wet now. There's something hungry and playful in her expression that I can't look away from. Warmth spreads between my legs and I let my hands wander down, cupping her ass instead of her waist.

"Did this help?" she asks.

"This definitely helped."

She laughs. "I meant our conversation."

"Oh, yeah. That too," I say and then brush a piece of hair behind her ears, my expression more serious. "It did. I don't usually get my ego rattled so it's throwing off my game keeping up with you."

"Because I'm just so different and you've never met a girl like me," Emmy teases.

"I know you're fucking with me but I'm being serious. This really has felt like a great first date. It's been a lot of fun getting to know you. There are people I've gotten to know over the course of a longer period of time who aren't even half as memorable as you."

Emmy gazes into my eyes and we're quiet for a beat—a beat that feels way too long. I worry for a second that I said too much. But then, she leans in and kisses me. I return the favor easily.

When Emmy pulls away, she asks, "Are we being stereotypical lesbians right now?"

"Yes, absolutely," I say. "All that's missing is us spending the entire trip to San Fransisco together and then moving in as soon as we come back to Colorado. We'll adopt a dog the week after, I'm sure."

"Perfect. Marriage before our one year anniversary?"

"The only way to do it," I say and run my hands up her back. "I don't know if I've actually told you how funny I think you are. You're also very hot. It's a lot for me to process."

Emmy smirks playfully and I can genuinely tell for the first time since we met that she's embarrassed.

"What? No one's said that to you before?" I ask, half-teasing but also genuinely curious.

"Hot, yes. But funny—not really," she admits. "You just get me."

"Shut up," I say, laughing as she puts her hand dreamily to her chest like she's swooning.

Emmy laces her fingers through mine. "Can I be honest?"

"Always."

"I really want to have sex but more than anything right now, I want to go run around in the snow."

I laugh. "That is not at all what I thought you were going to say."

"We were so cooped up in the airport. I just want to, like, breathe some fresh air for a second. Run around. I know we just took a shower but I need a little something."

I nod, following along. In all honesty, all my brain is latching onto is *I really want to have sex*. If a hot girl who wants to have sex with me says jump, I'll at least consider. "Okay. Let's do it, then."

chapter nine

EMMY and I bundle up and then head outside. The hotel is still a mess but we cut through the chaos and head outside into a burst of cold air. It's the kind of cold that hurts a little bit to breathe but Emmy is right—it feels good to be out here.

I take a deep breath of fresh, non-airport air and roll my shoulders, followed by my neck. It's dark out here, going on almost eight p.m. on a late winter evening. The lights from the airport and hotel illuminate the area around us. There are long stretches of road and the tracks to the metro, but not much else. Looking out for miles and miles, there's nothing else. The mountains loom over us from a distance, nearly one hundred miles away but still so large.

"This way," Emmy says.

She leads me further away from the airport and further out where the snow hasn't been shoveled as carefully yet. Salt and frozen-over snow cracks beneath our feet as we walk.

"There's not really a good place for us to go," she admits. It's an earnest observation; there's nothing much to see or do out here.

"Maybe over there?" I offer. I gesture toward a plot of land that's just a strip leading to essentially roads and parking lots, but it's something. The snow is piled up and away from the roads. It's the filthy city kind of snow and it's way too tall for us to climb, but we can at least see snow.

"There are so many beautiful places in Colorado to get stuck and this is where we end up," Emmy says.

I laugh. "What do you mean?"

"The odds of getting snowed in somewhere in Colorado in the winter is, like, never zero, right? Like, storms will blow through. Whatever. But us getting trapped specifically here is so funny to me," she says. She turns to me. "I've never been snowed in anywhere, so I think I'm taking it personally that it happened here. Like, I went out to Breckenridge last year in the winter and there was snow but nothing like this."

"You *wanted* to be snowed in?" I tease.

"That feels like the kind of place it should happen. Having it happen at the airport is so lame. I'd much rather get stuck somewhere that's, like, *cozy* at least. Not here," she says. "It's like how I love a rainstorm as an excuse to stay in. Get cozy in bed, watch TV, lay around. The airport is the exact opposite of that. Getting stuck inside somewhere comfortable is kind of romantic."

"And this is...not," I say. It's been fun and sexy to get to know Emmy, but the airport doesn't exactly have an intimate air to it.

Emmy turns to me and throws her arms over my shoulder. "I think it's romantic," Emmy says. "In its own way."

I smile, holding her close to me to keep her warm. "Yeah, in a very special way. A *don't think about it too much* kind of way."

Emmy smiles up at me and I kiss her. It feels familiar now. There's no question that at least right now, in this moment, we both want each other. Kissing doesn't feel scary or daunting. It's the closest I've gotten to feeling like I'm in a relationship of any kind in an embarrassingly long time. Usually, even after a couple of hangouts, casual kissing and intimacy can still feel a little stiff. I can't tell if it's our personalities or just that we don't have much time together that's making Emmy and I move much faster than that.

"The snow seems pretty under control," I say. "At least for now."

"I think it's supposed to get bad again overnight. But hopefully things will be calm enough for us to be able to fly out. As long as the snow stops coming as heavily around midnight, I think we'll be fine. But I'm also not an expert."

Emmy turns to me. "I'm sorry about your friend's wedding."

"It's alright. I'm mostly just missing the pre-party stuff. Family time. That kind of thing," I say. "I've never been that close with mine, so I consider Hannah and her family to be more of my family than my parents. It's been hard having everyone moved out and scattered around the country. No one is ever in the same place at the same time. Even holidays aren't reliable anymore because travel is so expensive and work schedules can be so finicky. I'm fortunate I work remotely."

"Yeah, that's nice," Emmy says. "I get it. I feel like with being a student, my schedule is completely different from everyone else's. I have random breaks and also random periods, like finals, where I'm basically dead to the world. I can sort of be available to my friends who aren't in school but I feel like my work never stops. It's like an eighty-hour a week job where I can't even afford to have fun during my free time. Broke and tired."

"Damn."

"Yeah," she agrees. "I don't regret it, though. I love what I do. It'll probably never pay me that well but that's never been why I wanted to do it."

I smile a little bit, imagining Emmy hunched over her textbooks at the library. I can see her as the hot TA for a freshman class and as a student leading her dissertation research. I absolutely would've had a crush on her if we'd crossed paths in school.

I stop myself from saying what it is that I really want to say—that it seems like our schedules might actually be really agreeable with each other. I essentially set my own schedule around my deadlines, while Emmy is locked into a very specific, not nine-to-five specific routine.

I can't go there. The second I start thinking about it and imagining a place for her in my life, I have something to lose.

Emmy lets out a small sigh. "This is not the winter wonderland I was hoping it would be."

"Odd since that is usually exactly how the Denver Airport is typically described."

She snorts. "I'm just bored. I don't really want to be in San Francisco for an academic conference but I'd rather be here than waiting. I want to get the trip over with and be back home already." She turns and looks at me. "Not bored because of you. This has been the only not boring part of this. I've really enjoyed hanging out with you. I just want to get a move on."

"No, no, you're fine. Not taking personal offense at all."

She throws back her head and laughs, bumping her weight against mine. "Stop! I swear. I just meant I'm feeling...*restless*. Bored isn't even the right word. I hate flying and the anticipation is killing me. I was mentally prepared initially and now I'm starting to feel nervous again."

"It'll be totally fine," I say.

"Something that always eases the fears of those who are anxious."

I bite back a smile."Fair enough. I probably should want to leave more urgently but I'm pretty patient."

"Oh, yeah?"

I blush as if she can see through the half-truth. I wouldn't necessarily consider myself impatient when it comes to most things; I genuinely am able to take my time and recognize certain things are out of my control.

But when it comes to romance, patience is the hardest thing for me to control.

"I mean, yeah," I say, shyly now.

"Do you want to be patient with me?"

My lips perk up immediately without meaning to. I look out over the empty roads and the piles of snow. "Not necessarily."

"Should we go back upstairs, then? If you don't want to be patient?"

"Only so long as you want to."

"I do."

I take Emmy's hand in mine and realize it's freezing. I nearly jump back from surprise. "Jesus, dude."

Emmy laughs. "Sorry. I don't have pockets on this coat. I brought my light one because it's supposed to be warmer in California."

"Here," I say, taking her hands and lifting them under my jacket. Her hands are so cold I can feel them on my stomach through my shirt, but I don't mind.

She brings her arms around so her hands are pressed to my back and stands close to me. Just as we start getting comfortable, snow begins falling again. It's light at first, but it's quickly turning into that perfect ski snow. I can tell it's going to get heavy again quickly.

We tilt our heads up toward the snow. I lift my hands above us in an attempt to shield our faces from the falling flakes.

"Now it's the winter wonderland you've been looking for," I say.

Emmy turns and looks at me, her expression soft. She

presses our bodies together, holding me as close to her as she physically can, and kisses me. "Take me upstairs."

BACK UPSTAIRS, we barely make it through the door before Emmy is kissing me again. The door shuts behind us as I bring my hands to her face and brush my thumbs over her cheekbones. Her face sits perfectly in my palms. She unzips my jacket and I shake it off, letting it fall to the floor. I then reach for hers, listening to the sweet sound of the zipper falling and her clothes coming off.

I lead her toward the bed and we fall on it together, sinking into the hotel sheets. My hands roam her body freely, moving from her face down her torso to her waist. I move up her shirt and take in every inch of her bare skin that I can.

There's finally nothing holding us back now. There's no urge for either of us to take our time after having taken our time all day.

"Can I be corny for a second and say I can't believe this is actually happening?" I ask breathlessly as I reach for Emmy's sweatshirt and then shirt.

"The stars really aligned for us," she says. I gently toss her clothes to the side and kiss her neck. Emmy gasps and grips onto me as I move up toward her ear.

She grabs my shirt and yanks it over my head, revealing a sports bra that I use as a makeshift binder. She's gentle with me at first, taking in the smooth expanse of my skin. My nipples are hard unrelated to the cold and her touch makes goosebumps pop up all over my body.

"God, you are so hot," she whispers, almost like she's saying it more to herself than me.

I kiss her again as she holds onto me. I ease my knee between her legs and her back arches toward me, hungry for me. We both still have our pants on but I know that won't last long. I'm dying to get back to the place we'd reached in the bathroom and go even further beyond that. I want to taste her; I want to spend every single second we have together doing everything I can for her.

I move her hair away from her neck and kiss her neck, moving down toward her chest and her stomach. I bring my lips to her nipples and suck gently at first to gauge her response. When she puts her hand on the back of my head, I follow her lead and use more pressure. She gasps as my teeth lightly graze over her raised mounds.

I continue kissing down her stomach and then reach for her pants. She lifts her hips, already knowing what I'm trying to do. When I get her pants off and drop them to the floor, she pulls me right back toward her without a second thought.

I replace my knee with my hand, caressing my fingers over her underwear at first. I can feel that she's already wet, which in response makes me even wetter. I sometimes genuinely believe that giving feels even better than receiving. I don't always want someone to go down on me or get me off, but I will never say no to the opportunity to get a hot woman off.

From a position where I can see her face, I move her underwear to the side and slide my fingers along her slit. Emmy fights to keep her eyes open but I can see from her expression that they're closing out of bliss. Her mouth is open and she's keeping a firm grip on my arm, her nails digging into my skin.

"Oh, fuck," Emmy moans.

"Like that?" I ask, using my thumb against her clit. She's already wet and only getting wetter by the second. It's taking everything in me to not duck my head and go straight into eating her out. But I want to hold onto some level of patience. I'll get there eventually; it doesn't have to be right now. This is a moment where I have patience.

Emmy's back arches toward me again. She rocks her hips against my thumb, silently telling me she wants more.

When I finally dip my fingers into her, she cries out from pleasure. "Oh my god," she says, almost like a sigh.

I start off gently at first, testing out what she likes. It doesn't take long for me to find the spots that make her writhe with pleasure. I curl my fingers inside of her and move slowly, caressing her g-spot. I can feel in the way she's responding that it's working for her. She laces her fingers through mine and grips tightly.

Hovering above her, I take in every detail of her. She's completely in the throes of it, her eyes closed and mouth open as she moans. She looks so beautiful; I can't even believe I'm here with her right now.

My eyes trail down her body, taking in the way her body moves against my fingers and the way she's reaching for the sheets. Her body is perfect—soft and warm. I could have sex with her a million times over looking at this view and it would never get boring.

I lower myself down and bring her closer to the edge of the bed. She reaches for my hair as I put her legs on either side of my head. Her nails and fingers are gentle against my scalp. She pulls just the tiniest bit against the short strands.

I start slowly at first, kissing her opening. She spreads her legs further for me and I dip my tongue against her, taking in her taste. She pants and moans, gripping harder onto my hair. It's the sweetest sound I've ever heard. It makes me want more from her; I want to see how loud and out of control I can make her feel.

I drag my tongue slowly over her clit and her hips buck against my face. I use my arms to hold her legs in place and increase my speed and pressure, trying to find the exact place that'll bring her to the edge.

"Harper," she moans. "Oh, my god. *Harper.*"

She grips my hair tightly and brings her hips tighter to my mouth. When I can tell she's getting close, I bring my fingers to her slit and slowly ease inside of her. She gasps in such a satisfying way that I feel like *I* could finish just from how much I'm enjoying the show.

Using my tongue and hands at the same time, I decide to bring her to the edge this time instead of teasing it out. She's soaking wet. I can taste her all over my tongue, my lips. My fingers are covered in her.

Emmy is panting and moaning in a voice that barely even sounds like her. Her eyes are closed, completely lost in the sensation. I keep my eyes fixed on what I can see of her—her gripping her breasts and the hard line of her jaw as she opens her mouth to moan.

"I'm gonna cum," she moans out. She's completely breathless and it's so fucking hot. I want to tell her this but I'm too focused on the task at hand. I don't want to move my mouth away until she cums in it.

Emmy suddenly goes quiet, her body tensing. She presses her thighs to the sides of my face and then cries out. "Oh my god," she says. Her body relaxes and her legs start shaking. When I slide my fingers out of her, her body shivers in response. Her chest rises and falls with her breath.

I get up from the spot I'd settled onto on the floor and join her on the bed. She reaches for me, pulling me close. I lay down and open my arms to her so she can lay on me.

Emmy rests her head on my chest, both of us laying in silence. Emmy has goosebumps all over her skin.

"Are you just really moved by the sex we had or are we cold?" I whisper, leaning my head against hers.

"A little bit of both but mostly cold," she says and I nod.

We move under the covers and rest our heads on the cushy hotel pillows. It's freezing outside but there's nothing cold about our hotel room. Between sex and now the comforter, my body is covered in a thin sheen of sweat.

After a little bit of laying together, Emmy sits up and lifts her hair from her neck. She turns and looks back at me over her shoulder. It's the kind of look that takes my breath away. "That was…" she says and then starts laughing. "That was insane. I feel like I legitimately need to thank you."

I laugh and put my hand on her exposed lower back. I drag my thumb across her skin absent-mindedly. "No need to thank me. I feel like I should be thanking you for the opportunity to begin with."

"Oh, please," she says and then laughs again, rolling her eyes.

I sit up next to her and wrap my arms around her waist. "It's true. It was an honor. And a privilege." I kiss her forehead and Emmy leans into it, letting her weight rest against me. "Do you need anything? Water? Snacks?"

"Actually both sound so good right now," Emmy admits. She starts to get up and I push up from the bed so I can get up before her.

"No, it's okay. I can grab it."

"Are you sure?"

"Yeah, I got it. I don't mind," I say. I readjust my boxers and walk over to the hotel mini fridge. I squat down the floor to see what's inside. There isn't much but some waters and bagged snacks, and then a little note.

"What's that?" Emmy asks as I pull out the piece of paper.

"It's a note from the hotel telling us the stuff in here is complementary. But there are more snacks downstairs in case we need food," I say and shrug. "Any preference for snacks?"

"Whatever's in there. Something sweet if they have it."

"You got it," I say. I pull out two waters and a bag of cookies and then stand up, I crack open both of the bottles before handing one over to Emmy.

"Thank you," she says as she takes it.

We sip our waters in comfortable silence. Everything feels weirdly familiar but also extremely surreal. I can't get my brain to actually believe that this is happening at the same time that I'm *very* present in my body. I don't want to overstate it and scare her off, but this is definitely the best one night stand—or whatever this is—I've ever had. I've never experienced that kind of chemistry with someone. The chemistry has been palpable the entire time we've been together but this is a whole other level. This confirms the chemistry is there.

But that's also objectively insane of me to think and feel right now. We've had sex once and I don't know this girl. It could be any number of factors that have made this feel borderline magical—including that there's a time constraint and there's been so much build-up to this moment.

I look at Emmy from her spot in the bed and try to figure out what she's thinking from her expression. Her eyes are focused on the open bag of cookies in her hand, so I can't get much of a read. I can only hope that her review was a genuine one and it really was that good for her.

Emmy finishes her bag of cookies and gets up, tossing the empty bag in the trash. She grabs a shirt from the ground—my shirt—and pulls it over her naked body. It sits on her frame differently than it does on me despite the fact that our builds aren't that different. She's shorter and thinner where I'm more muscular. Her legs are long and lean.

She sips her water effortlessly and places it down on the hotel dresser near her. "Hi," she says.

"You look better in that than I do," I say, unable to pull my eyes away. She giggles and turns away, shaking her head. "What, you're suddenly feeling shy?" I tease.

"Maybe," she says and then walks over to me. She twists her mouth in a way that is so irresistably cute it takes everything in me to not scoop her in my arms and kiss her a million times.

She beats me to it, draping her arms around my neck and then kissing me. Even though she's wearing my shirt, it feels softer and better on her. It's just a plain t-shirt but I like it so much more all the sudden.

As we kiss, her hands travel over my shoulders and down my back, brushing over the material of my sports bra.

"Did you want anything?" Emmy asks, looking up at me through her eyelashes.

"Me?" I ask, blushing because I'm apparently an idiot who has never had sex with a woman before this moment. My complete lack of game surprises even me. "Oh. I mean..."

"Obviously no pressure, but if you want..." she says, raising her eyebrows slightly.

I think of the wetness between my legs, currently pooled in my boxers. I think of how gentle her hands are and how hot she is and how I've felt so comfortable with her. I love being here with her. It's unusual for me.

"I don't typically...receive," I say, which is the honest truth. "I've always been more of a giver, I guess."

"That's okay, we don't *have* to do anything. I just want to make sure you know it's an option in case you want it."

"I should've known you'd know the exact right thing to say," I admit.

"Oh? Why is that?"

"You're just so *nice*. And gentle. I was just thinking about how comfortable I feel with you and how nice this has all been. I don't typically like to receive because I have to feel safe enough to," I say, "or whatever."

"Or whatever," Emmy echoes, teasing me slightly. "You don't have to downplay it. I also think you're nice and gentle and I feel comfortable with you. I'm glad you feel the same way."

"Comfortable enough to really want you," I say.

Emmy stops and looks at me, her eyes locking with mine. Heat rises between us in an instant as we both realize what it is we're thinking. As soon as I say the words, I realize how true it is and how suddenly impatient I'm feeling.

"Tell me what you like," Emmy says. She steps closer to me until we're touching. Her hands find my lower back. "What makes you feel comfortable?"

For the first time in a long time—or maybe ever—I feel so incredibly...feminine. I've always been more masculine, both in attitude and the way I dress. I'm direct with the people I'm flirting with and usually take charge of the situation. My type tends to lean more femme and it's not to say they don't offer, but it's rare for someone our first night having sex to offer to get me off. And it's even rarer for me to genuinely want them to get me off. My preference has always been to focus on their pleasure and what they want; it's just as enjoyable to me as someone getting me off, sometimes even more enjoyable.

But I find my brain saying *yes, yes, yes* to the option of Emmy touching me. There's not an ounce of hesitation.

"I prefer to keep my sports bra on," I say.

Emmy nods. It all feels extremely hot instead of somewhat clinical like some conversations around sex can be. "Easy. We can do that." She keeps her voice low, sexy. It makes me weak at the knees.

"I don't really like penetration that much."

"Okay. Also easy for me to follow."

She leans in and gently kisses my neck. Warmth rushes south and my knees nearly go weak. "I like that," I whisper.

Emmy hums a sound of acknowledgement against my throat and I hold her close to me, gripping onto her shirt. She presses me up against the hotel room desk. I don't really recognize myself—it's been a long time since I've been the one in this position—but I'm really liking it. It's hot that Emmy wants to take charge. Her heart genuinely seems in it and it's turning me on even more than I would typically be turned on.

She brings her hand up my thighs and then between my legs, touching me over my boxers. "What about that?"

My brain feels like radio static in the best way imaginable. "Yes," I say, hardly able to get the word out. I grip onto her and spread my legs wider. "I like that."

She drags a finger over my slit, toying with me. It feels so good that it nearly takes my breath away. She leans her weight against me and locks eyes with me as she uses her hands. I'm entirely at ease, making it possible for me to completely lose myself to the feeling. I've never been one to fake an orgasm, but I will pretend it's better than it is if the situation calls for it. Fortunately, this situation definitely won't be calling for it.

"Fuck." I exhale and Emmy places her face near mine to listen to my increasingly rapid breath.

She moves her hands expertly, knowing exactly what to do. She's so in tune with every breath, every movement. She knows what will pull a reaction out of me. I like that she's a quick learner.

Emmy brushes her fingers over my clit and my brain completely fries out. I can't produce a logical thought, can't speak, can hardly even make a sound. I grip onto her, completely lost in how good her hands feel on me.

I rock my hips against her and hold tightly onto her as the orgasm rushes over me. It burns fast, leaving me no time for build-up. Before I know it, I'm panting in Emmy's ear and full-body flushed in the way that only happens after finishing during sex.

I rest my head against Emmy's shoulder to catch my breath. "Wow," I say and then laugh a little bit.

Emmy presses her lips to my temple. "How was that?" she asks, her voice still low.

"That was...perfect," I say, because it feels way too forward to tell her it's the best I've probably ever had. No, actually–it *is* the best I've ever had.

She laughs and kisses down my face, soft and gentle just like her hands. "I'm so glad."

Our phones disrupt our moment. They go off simultaneously from the nightstand nearby and I nearly groan. I want to bask in this moment a little bit longer. I'm really enjoying the afterglow.

"I think it's probably about our flight if it's both of our phones," Emmy says.

"Right," I say, knowing I should check it. But I'm reluctant. I don't want this moment to end. Our flights signal the inevitable beginning of the end; we'll have to leave here. We can't stay forever, even though I want to.

She walks over to the nightstand and retrieves our phones. She then brings mine back to me as she looks at her own screen. "It is—we've been rebooked for tomorrow. First flight out," she says. "You're booked on the same one, right?"

I don't want to read too much into her tone and the panic around the possibility that we might not be on the same flight. My heart thuds and I'm anxious all over again about all of this. I can't tell if I'm overthinking or if I'm missing obvious signals from her. It feels like it could be either. She has a fear of flying, who's to say she's not just looking for a friend to make flying feel less scary tomorrow?

"I am," I say, somewhat reluctantly.

"So we're supposed to fly out in, like, six hours." Emmy twists her mouth with what seems like it might be disappointment. "I guess we should get some sleep. We both have big days tomorrow."

"Right," I agree, trying not to make it obvious that I'm bummed. But I'm not ready for this to be over. I don't want to have to be responsible and get a full night of sleep; I want to spend all night fooling around with Emmy and getting to know her. But I can take the hint if she doesn't feel the same way. We technically both got what we wanted. It would be silly of me to think that I should also expect emotional connection from what's been consistenly flirty and casual.

I pull up my text chain with Hannah. *Coming to you early tomorrow,* I write and then attach a screenshot of my rebooked flight information.

Hannah's text bubble pops up almost immediately. I don't even have the chance to lock my phone. *Are you with her???*

I smile a little bit, glancing up at Emmy. She's also texting, both of us distracted for the moment. Even so, I tilt my phone away from her just the tiniest bit so I don't risk her seeing. *You're not going to believe the night I just had.*

I NEED TO KNOW EVERYTHING.

Shouldn't you be asleep by now? I respond.

I was waiting to hear updates from you. Mostly about your wild airport fling but also about when you're arriving for my wedding or whatever.

I let out a laugh through my nose. *I'll tell you the details tomorrow.*

Write everything down so you don't forget a single detail.

I don't have to write a single second of this down. I already know I'll remember every bit of it forever, I write back without hesitation.

Now I really need to meet her.

I smile a little bit, thinking about Hannah and Emmy meeting. I don't know Emmy well, but it seems like they'd get along.

I'll text you in the morning when I'm on my way.

Kiss her for me!

I put my phone down and look at Emmy, who then puts her phone down. "Should we get ready for bed?" I ask, because that's the easier thing to say than telling her I want to keep spending time with her even if it means I'll be sleep-deprived tomorrow.

"Okay," Emmy agrees.

We get ready in our own ways, Emmy setting up her night-stand with water and charging her phone. She pulls a retainer case out of her backpack. I just throw myself into bed, setting an alarm for myself to give enough time to get through TSA tomorrow.

"It's kind of nice to be so close to the airport. I feel like we can leave, like, twenty minutes before boarding and still get there on time," I say.

"Oh, I could never risk it. I have too much anxiety around flying. It's like I have to memorize the entire interior of the airport before I can comfortably wait for boarding."

I snort and push away the feeling that that means she might get up several hours before me. The thought of waking up alone in the hotel room makes my chest feel tight. "Right," I say, trying to sound casual.

We settle into bed and I resist the urge to ask Emmy when she set her alarms for. I'll probably hear them, so I'll probably be able to get away with getting up with her then.

"Can I...?" Emmy asks, moving close to me.

"Of course," I say. I know I'm doing a bad job of hiding how excited I am, but I don't care. A hot girl wants to cuddle with me; I have all the reason in the world to be excited.

She turns the light off, making the room go completely dark. She then snuggles in close, laying on my chest.

chapter ten

I WAKE up with a start to my phone alarm blaring from my nightstand. I blink a couple of times, trying to place where I am and when I would've fallen asleep. When I check my phone, it's only about two hours after the last time I checked my phone. It's probably the worst night of sleep I've ever gotten outside of some long nights in college, but I can't bring myself to care.

Emmy and I are completely interwoven. Her head is resting on my chest and our arms and legs are a tangled mess. I want to stay here for as long as I can; I could do an entire day of laying like this without moving. I want to order in room service and have sex and cuddle and sleep.

But real life is waiting for us. We have a flight to catch. I have a wedding to get to and Emmy has her conference.

"Emmy," I whisper. I nudge her gently, barely moving her. I don't really know her, so I don't know how she's going to act to being woken up. I slide out from under her and she reaches for me.

"Do we have to get up?" she asks. Her voice is low and sweet with sleep. Her eyes are still closed. "You can't make me get up."

I laugh and fall back into bed with her. I wrap her in my arms and she sleepily lays in them. "I'm sorry. I really am."

She moans playfully, moving further under the comforter. "I can't do it. No flight today. At least you're flying out for something fun. I'm just going to be at a conference with a bunch of people who would much rather be sightseeing than listening to PowerPoint presentations."

"'Something tells me you love those PowerPoint presentations."

Emmy peeks out from under the comforter, finally opening her eyes. "Okay, maybe I do."

"It'll be fun, I swear. As much as I want to hangout here and put off leaving, we don't have much time to get ready for our flight. We'll probably get the *boarding soon* text in a little bit."

"I can't believe I have to get on a plane," she says. After a second, she finally throws the comforter off and gets up.

I follow suit, pulling clothes for the day out of my suitcase. Emmy yawns as she gets dressed. She hands my t-shirt over to me and I put it in my suitcase along with my other dirty clothes from yesterday.

We move around the hotel room in a way that feels familiar, like we've been doing this forever. Everything is done in silence but it's comfortable and easy. We head to the bathroom together to brush our teeth and spend the whole time touching each other in passing. It feels so different from anyone I've ever dated previously.

I look at Emmy through the mirror, wondering what she's thinking. I'm trying so hard to not get caught up in everything—the anxiety of if we'll ever see each other again and wondering if any of this actually meant anything. But it's hard the closer the end of our time together gets. Reality is setting in and it's not feeling particularly welcome.

As time goes on, the comfortable feeling between us

begins to fade. Is the way Emmy putting her sweater on meant to signify to me that she has no interest in seeing me again? Is she brushing her teeth thinking about how she'll never have to see me again after this? Maybe already thinking about her next trip where she'll be able to do this with someone else?

We then go on to pack in the kind of quiet that only amplifies my anxiety. What probably would've felt comfortable last night now feels debilitating. I have no idea what to say to her. It's like all of our previous conversations have meant nothing and I haven't retained a single thing. I can't think of a single reasonable topic, not even stupid small talk. My mind is so completely and entirely blank.

I know it's just me. I'm the one working myself up. The only reason I feel weird is because of things I'm entirely making up in my head. Nothing in the way she's speaking to me or moving around the hotel room suggests she feels different.

"Emmy," I say suddenly, surprising myself. My mouth goes dry. I can't believe I set myself up like this. When she turns to me, I know that I have to commit.

"Yeah?" she asks, stopping what she's doing.

I can't look at her. She's too beautiful, too kind, too funny. All of it radiates off of her in a way that's almost blinding. I'm forced to stare at my feet and the wall behind her head and our bags in the corner of the room. "I—"

She walks over to me, giving me her full, undivided attention. We're both definitely in a rush and this isn't the time to stall. But I also know that this is the time that I have to say what's on my mind. Right now is the time to be grown up about this.

"I'd like to see you again. Outside of this," I say, fighting the hot blush spreading over my entire body. I've never felt so vulnerable ever in my life. "Maybe when we're both home from our trips."

Emmy is quiet for a second and I realize then with a crushing weight to my chest that this has never been serious to her. I completely misread the situation.

She tilts my face up toward hers with just her fingertips, forcing me to look at her. "You want to keep seeing me again?" she asks quietly, her lips turning up in a slight smile.

"I would, yeah," I say. "It's true what I said about going on a second date with you if we'd met on a dating app. This has been really...fun. I've liked getting to know you. More than most people I've been on a date with, like, ever."

Emmy steps even closer to me and then wraps her arms around my neck. She presses her body to mine.

"You want to be my airport crush?" Emmy teases.

"I want *you* to be *my* airport crush," I say and she laughs.

"Done and done," she says. "On both fronts. On all fronts. I'll see you next week."

She wraps her arms around my neck and kisses me—deeply, passionately, like she knows we'll have exactly this forever.

It's perfect.

about the author

Josie Mae (she/her) writes small town-adjacent lesbian &
queer romance from her not-so-small town. She un-ironically
says yeehaw despite being a city girl and spends most of her
time daydreaming about wide open spaces (and being swept
off her feet by a cowgirl).

You can connect with her on:
Instagram: @josiemaebooks
TikTok: @josiemaebooks